W9-CCW-967

ONE SMALL HOP

ONE SMALL HOP

MADELYN ROSENBERG

Scholastic Press / New York

Library of Congress Cataloging-in-Publication Data available

ISBN 978-1-338-56561-4

1 2021

Printed in the U.S.A. 23

First edition, May 2021

Book design by Baily Crawford

For Graham and Karina, as always

CHAPTER 1

Seventh grade is a series of multiple-choice questions. I'm not just talking about quizzes or choices in the school cafeteria, which are more like choices between types of torture than types of food.

I'm talking transportation. Do you: (A) walk, or (B) ride your bike? (Bike.)

I'm talking ethics. Do you: (A) tell your middle school principal that her records are completely vulnerable, or (B) hack them? (Hack, though Davy is better at it than I am.)

I'm also talking personal safety. Do you: (A) take Davy's bet and wade along Blue Harbor's toxic shoreline or (B) avoid it like the plague? (Take the bet. And I didn't get the plague or even toe fungus. But I did get a weird respiratory thing that kept me out of school for two weeks. Davy blamed himself, for mentioning it.)

Social situations require more letters of the alphabet.

For instance, say it's a Friday afternoon and you witness your so-called friends hanging out with your so-called enemy. Do you:

(A) Pretend it doesn't bug you that your friends are talking to Derek Ripley, a guy who's hated you since second grade?

(B) Keep walking and pretend you don't see them?

(C) Go right up to them and ask why they're even hanging out with Derek Ripley when they know he still calls you Slime Boy?

Strategically, B has worked for me the most often, so I stepped into the courtyard and stared up at the clouds, which were white and fluffy but still somehow ominous against the painted afternoon sky.

This is not a metaphor: The sky was literally painted on the underside of the awning that covered every centimeter of the courtyard at Blue Harbor Middle School. The awning was supposed to protect us from what Principal Brown called "The Elements." Basically, it meant that school authorities had decided the best way to preserve student health was to put up the equivalent of a giant umbrella.

"Yo, Goldstein." Derek noticed me first. His voice was tough and low, as if he was trying out for Detective No. 2 in the school play.

I pretended I was shocked and surprised to see them all standing there. "Yo," I said, even though I'm not the *yo* type.

"Did you hear?" Derek said. "Varney found a lobster."

"So?" We were always finding lobsters, or pieces of them, along the banks of what we still called Blue Harbor. The original harbor was washed out before I was born, when the ocean swelled up and swallowed half our town—and every other town along the East Coast. It moved our shoreline to where Main Street used to be. We could see slabs of pavement below the surface when the sand shifted, which was pretty much all the time. There were still calm spots, but the waves mostly came at the shore like they were looking for a fight.

Sometimes the waves brought shells with them, or lobster claws, always detached. I had a jar of them at home, dry and light as dust.

"*So?*" Derek mimicked. "You wouldn't say that if you knew what I knew."

"Oh, just tell him, Derek," said Delphinium Perez, her face glowing, her mouth looking like it wanted to tell. Under normal circumstances, Delphinium would have told—she talked to me more than any other girl in Blue Harbor, including my own sister. But Derek was king of the moment. I walked toward him, a magnet compelled, and I understood why my two best friends had stopped to listen. I almost forgave them: Delphinium with her skinny arms and sneaky smile, and Davy Hudson, who memorized Latin phrase books and was shorter than everyone else because he'd skipped a grade. I could have skipped a grade, too, but my mother didn't want me to be too far away from what she called my "socially correct peer group." I pictured the seventh graders

I knew. There wasn't anything socially correct about a single one of us.

"Just tell me, Derek," I repeated. "What's the big deal?"

"It's alive!" Davy crowed, forgetting all about Derek's kingly status.

"For real?"

"For real, Slime Boy. It was moving its claws and everything. I'll bet it weighed a pound and a half."

"Is that a lot?" asked Delphinium. She had been named, like her sisters, after New England's recently extinct wildflowers. Indigo was the luckiest in her family; Lupine, which sounded like the scientific name for "port-a-potty," came off the worst.

"It weighs more than a softball," I said. Despite her skinny arms, Delph pitched for the school softball team. Davy liked to calculate her ERA, which was currently at 1.89. "More like three softballs. That'd be the equivalent of 680 grams."

"I know what a pound and a half is, thank you," said Delphinium, who was also good at math. I kept trying to get her (and everyone else) to use the metric system, like every other country in the world. No luck. "I meant: Is that a lot *for a lobster*?"

"Anything's a lot for a lobster, if it's alive." I looked at Derek. "You're sure Leroy wasn't joking? He wasn't just wiggling it around?"

"I saw it myself," Derek said. "I held it. Almost got pinched, too. Had to get all the details for my dad."

Derek's father worked for the EPF, which officially stood for Environmental Police Force. Unofficially, it stood for Police Farce. And sometimes Police Farts. They were a government agency, sort of new and already corrupt, set up to satisfy a group of scientists who were still worried about climate change.

I suppose I should be glad that the government had finally acknowledged that the climate *was* changing, and had been, faster than anybody had imagined. When my dad was my age, the government said it was all a lie. Which may be one reason that he could never get used to the new restrictions, which, okay, were probably created so the EPF could give out fines. Those were used to give bonuses to the EPF workers so they could take their families on nice vacations. They didn't seem to be using the money to fund research or do anything that would make the environment better.

Along with issuing fines, the EPF had a game division, which transported "fragile species," a designation that made it sound like it was the animals' fault they were dying, to the Center for Species Rehabilitation in New Arcadia. Our science class was supposed to take a virtual field trip there. Mr. Kletter, our science teacher, had already suggested that we "manage our expectations."

"Does Leroy still have it?" I gave up trying to hide my excitement.

"Doubt it," Derek said. "I told my dad as soon as I put the thing back in the bucket. He's probably bringing Varney to headquarters right now. The Blue Harbor EPF has the most efficient—"

I was already halfway to my bike. "Come on!" I was addressing my actual friends, but Derek went for his bicycle, too. I pulled my One out of my pocket, mounted it on my handlebars, and said Leroy Varney's name. A projection beamed back at me, mapping my way to his house. Left on Rockaway, right on Gull, that was the shortest route. It took us away from the town's air-conditioned bike path, but I didn't care.

"No fair, Ahab." Davy pedaled hard behind me. His hair was cut short and close, in a fade, but that didn't stop the sweat from dripping down his neck. "Ever hear of breathing?"

I pedaled harder and held straight for two more blocks until Beacon, my own sweat coating my chest like oil. Heat rose from the pavement and blurred the horizon. Every now and then, we passed a yard that looked lush and green, as if it had come out of a catalog, which it probably had. The other yards were ashy brown. Spring in Maine. What a joke.

I'd heard my mother wax poetic about the springs of her childhood, where people hunted for snowdrops or the first purple crocus. You'd have to be blind, deaf, and anosmic to think that this—the code reds and an ocean that the media had nicknamed the New Dead Sea—was the way the world was supposed to be. But that's the world I pedaled through to get to Leroy's.

CHAPTER 2

Leroy Varney's house was painted green and took up most of a scrubby lot on Beacon Street. Even if I hadn't had the address, it was easy to tell which house was his: There were two EPF scooters parked out front.

The door opened and Officer Ripley and his partner came out, carrying a metal tank between them. Leroy was nowhere in sight.

"That's my dad," Derek said. I was glad he was out of breath, too.

It was easy to tell Officer Ripley and Derek were related. They had the same squarish head; the same blue eyes, close-set, like the eyes of a (now-extinct) possum; and the same short brown hair. Officer Ripley had a small dent in his chin, which made him look more like a movie cop than a real one.

"D," Officer Ripley said. "Don't you know better than to bring an audience when we're conducting official police business?" He laughed to show he was joking and nodded at his partner. Together, they set the tank on the ground near their feet. I felt sorry for the lobster, trapped in the dark.

"I was seeing if you followed up on my tip," Derek said.

Officer Ripley beamed. "Going to join the EPF in no time, this one," he said. "If you're not careful, CJ, he's going to take over as my partner. You remember my son, Derek?"

"Of course." His partner's blond hair was pulled back so tightly that her forehead could have ripped apart at any moment. Like Officer Ripley, she wore a green uniform with a badge. Her name tag said SILVA.

Officer Ripley nodded at his son. "These your friends?"

Derek paused a beat too long. "They're from school," he said finally.

"Well, go on. Make your introductions."

Derek fused our names together so they sounded like one big, long one: Ahabgoldsteindavidhudsondelphiniumperez.

"Goldstein." Officer Ripley checked out my curly hair and black-framed glasses. "Your father's Ted Goldstein?"

Unlike Davy, I'd just had a growth spurt, so I was about the same height as my dad. I was also fifty kilograms lighter. Sometimes it was hard to tell we were related. "Yes," I said.

"Him I know. Your usage alarm's gone off about twenty times in the last three weeks; are you aware of that?"

"Not exactly." I shifted my weight—fifty-four kilograms—from one foot to the other. The thing was, those were almost the same words *I* used when I talked to my father, except I started the sentence with "Dad."

Dad, you're not supposed to throw that away.

Dad, we've used up our meat allowance.

Dad, the alarm's going off again.

DAD!

Of course our alarm was going off. My dad overused water, power, and everything else you could possibly overuse. I knew it every time the shower cut off before my allotted two minutes were up. I knew it because of the stack of green tickets—paper, because the EPF was either stupid or ironic—stacked on top of his desk. I'd heard that alarm, with its police-siren wail so that the whole neighborhood knew exactly who was sucking up too much energy and who was throwing super-juice pouches into the garbage instead of the recycling shoot.

"He still have that behemoth in your garage?" Officer Ripley went on.

"Yes," I said. "But he doesn't drive it. I swear."

The behemoth was my dad's Suburban Utility Vehicle, or SUV, and it sat inside what would have been the world's greatest lab space. Instead, the garage was taken up by a vehicle my dad referred to as *Helluva Car*, which he was only allowed to drive in the Fourth of July parade. Aside from the obvious shortage of gasoline, the SUV—or Soov, as Davy called it—violated something like fifty thousand emissions regulations.

"They don't make them like this anymore," my dad had said more than once, thumping the hood with his fist.

"I could do a lot with this garage," I said. I pictured the shelf with microscope slides and test tubes instead of his emergency cans of gasoline.

"Like what?"

"Inventions. Experiments." With so much room, anything seemed possible, like making a discovery big enough to get me into Darwin's Disciples. It sounded like a gang, and it was, in a way: a gang of scientists. A secret society. People didn't talk about the Disciples openly, but I knew enough to know that I wanted to be one. If I got in, I'd receive an invitation on a green card with gold lettering. I'd be one of the youngest to make it, and if I did make it, my future would be wide open.

"You can do experiments in your room," my dad said.

"Not with wildlife or chemicals." My mom had rules about what I could bring inside the house. Things with Heartbeats were at the top of her ABSOLUTELY FORBIDDEN list, just under Things that Exploded.

"The garage is mine," my dad said. "You wait. These regulations aren't going to stick. Someday I'll be able to drive this baby wherever I want."

My dad was convinced his time would come again. Either we'd go back to a government that didn't believe the world was dying or we'd get a bunch of scientists who'd fix it. Maybe they'd invent a space vacuum to hoover up the greenhouse gases or come up with some sort of industrial wet vac to suck up toxic algae blooms. Someone, a Disciple probably, would fill the earth with oil again, inject it like Botox and coat it with moisturizer.

Then Ted Goldstein would pull his Soov out of the garage and drive it more than once a year. He'd eat twenty-dollar burgers and take showers that steamed up the bathroom. I wasn't sure what was so great about being able to write your name on a fogged-up bathroom mirror, but it would be nice to be in a world where you could ride your bike in the street without the hot wind coming at you like a blast of bad breath.

Officer Ripley was still talking. I pushed my glasses against my nose and waited for the end of the lecture. I hoped he'd mistake my silence for respect. "—everyone's responsibility," he said finally. "Maybe you can talk some sense into him."

"I can try," I said. I *had* tried. "Officer Ripley? May we see the lobster, sir?" His jaw unlocked. I'd been right to add the "sir."

"I don't see why not," he began, but his partner interrupted.

"We have to get back, Rip." She reached down to pick up the tank again, but Officer Ripley put his foot on it to stop her.

"For educational purposes, CJ," he said, stooping down. "For the kids."

We crowded around the tank, even Derek, who had

already seen the thing. I held my breath as Officer Ripley lifted the lid.

The lobster was bigger than anything I'd seen washed up on the shores of Blue Harbor. His neck, if lobsters had necks, was spotted, his claws parted, his fanlike tail curled under. He sat stock-still, like he was waiting for something. Then I noticed his antennae. Instead of standing rigid and alert, like in pictures, they were wilted. That meant he was:

(A) sleeping,

(B) scared,

(C) sick, or

(D) dead.

Please be B, I thought. *Or A. B or A.*

There was a pump in the tank, but it wasn't making any bubbles.

"Some monster," I said. "I thought he almost pinched you, Derek."

"He did. He was snapping like he wanted a piece of me." Derek reached out and pinched me on the arm. "Like this." He looked at his dad. "What happened to it?"

"Hard to keep a creature like this alive without the proper transportation device," Officer Ripley said. "Delicate boogers. No constitution. It was a miracle the Varney kid found it alive in the first place. You hope for the best, expect the worst."

"So he's dead?" I asked.

"Course he's dead. Your friend didn't know how to properly maintain it. Carried it home in a bucket. May as well have been a coffin."

"Rip, we really have to—" Officer Silva began.

"Hold on, just hold on. This is a teaching moment. Kids, what do you do if you're walking by the edge of the harbor and you happen to spot something like our lobster friend, still kicking? Anyone?"

"We call a certified member of the EPF!" Derek recited.

"Do you touch it?" Officer Silva asked, getting in the spirit of things.

"No," Derek said.

"Do you put it in a *stinking bucket*?" Officer Ripley asked.

I hadn't taken my eyes off the dead lobster, but I noticed the effort it took for Officer Ripley to use a sanitized word like *stinking*, when a thousand other words must have been going through his head.

"No, sir!" Derek barked, right on cue. "Pursuant to environmental code RE 248: When a fragile or near-fragile species is spotted in the wild, do not touch said species without consulting a fully trained EPF specialist."

"And do you go into the water?"

"No, sir."

"I didn't hear the rest of you. I said: 'Do you go into the water?'"

Derek crossed his arms like his father and waited.

"No, sir," Davy piped up.

"Miss?"

"No," Delphinium answered.

I didn't take my eyes away from the dead lobster as I chose my words. "You don't go into the water."

I said it so slowly that Officer Ripley must have wondered if my brain was getting enough oxygen. But when I looked up, he smiled and punched his partner in the shoulder. "See what I mean?" he said. "Teaching moment." He put the lid back in place and strapped the tank on the back of his scooter. To Derek he said, "See you at home, D." Then he pressed his thumb against the ignition disk, gunned his motor once for effect—a weak effect, given that the environmentally sound DM-400 made about as much noise as a coughing mosquito—and drove away with Officer Silva.

"Now what?" asked Davy.

"Now we go see Leroy," I said.

CHAPTER 3

"The Lobster Killer?" Derek said. "Nice company."

"It's a condolence call," I said.

"Maybe for you. I'm out of here."

Good, I thought. I didn't make a move toward the house until Derek disappeared, down the air-conditioned bike path this time, and riding slower.

"I suppose Leroy *has* suffered a loss," Davy said. He made his face funereal, which wasn't so different from his usual expression. I led the way with Davy and Delph behind me, points on a triangle. Leroy opened the door before we reached his front steps.

"Hi," I said.

"I was watching you. Wasn't sure you'd knock."

"Why wouldn't we?"

"You might not want to be seen talking to me after what happened." Leroy's eyes searched ours. He didn't mention that we'd never been seen talking to him before this happened, either. It was a big school and we only knew each other vaguely.

"Oh, come on," Delphinium told him in her I'm-going-into-foreign-relations-someday voice. "Give yourself a break. It wasn't your fault."

I gave her the side-eye. "Whose fault was it, then?"

"It was . . . circumstances."

"You don't have to be nice about it. I know I killed it," Leroy said. His hair fell over his eyes.

"It still would have died if you'd left it where it was," Delphinium said. "They always do. It could have happened to anyone."

"It wouldn't have happened to Ahab," Leroy said.

True, I probably could have kept that lobster alive for longer. I'd been studying habitats and life cycles—marine and otherwise—for as long as I could remember. And while I didn't have much of a lab, I had a couple of aquariums outfitted with aeration systems. I had more than a bucket. Still, Delph was right: The lobster probably wouldn't have lasted long anyway.

Leroy waited for me to pass judgment.

"Well," I said finally. "It's not like you *meant* to kill it." A court wouldn't have convicted him of lobster murder, just involuntary lobster slaughter.

Leroy gave me an almost smile.

"So where did you find him?" I asked. "What were you

going to do with him, once you got him home? Why would you let someone like Derek Ripley know you had him?"

"And how'd you get out of school so early?" added Davy. He was a rule follower in real life; it was just online that he broke them. Still, he liked to know how other people broke rules, in case he ever needed to do the same.

"Who are you? The EPF?" Leroy said. "I answered all those questions already."

"Not honestly," I said.

Now Leroy grinned with his whole mouth. I could see a slight gap between his front teeth.

"So what'd you tell them?" I asked.

"That I was walking along the shoreline and I saw something moving."

"What really happened?"

"I'm in enough trouble as it is."

"We won't tell," I said.

"Why do you want to know?" Leroy tapped his hands on his legs, but the beat wasn't random, it was organized, like a drum solo.

I wanted to know for the same reason the government wanted to know. Because this was *life*. Something was out there, something that wasn't floating belly up. And, okay, maybe it was dead *now*. But maybe there was another one that wasn't. Maybe we could find it and revive it, *unlike* the EPF, which couldn't keep a cockroach alive. Or wouldn't.

"Scientific curiosity?" I said.

Leroy thought for a minute. "I kind of wanted to tell somebody anyway. That's why I spilled it to Derek. Mistake Number One."

"Number Two."

"Hey, now," said Leroy.

I changed the subject. "So you didn't find it along the shore?"

"Nope."

"You didn't go *in*, did you?" Delphinium took a step back, as if she thought toxins would start oozing out of Leroy's skin.

"I took a boat," Leroy said.

I looked around the bare yard. "You don't own a boat." No one did; there was no point.

"I built one, for history class. A dugout canoe, like the Indigenous Americans. It didn't have to be life-size, but I thought if it was, Duckworth might give me extra credit."

Duckworth, I thought. Well, that explained a lot.

"I just wanted to see if it would float," he said.

"And it did?"

He nodded, the smile finally reaching his eyes. "I took her out during study hall. It's not like anything else was going on. I usually skip sixth period."

"That was very brave," Delphinium said. "Going out on the water alone." Leroy must have recognized the admiration in her voice, because he stood straighter until she added, "Stupid, but brave."

"And nobody saw you?" Davy was still looking for professional insight.

"She's small," Leroy said. "And she doesn't exactly look like a boat—more like a go-kart with missing wheels."

"Weren't you afraid that you'd fall in?" Delphinium asked, that tone still there.

"Nah, she's steady."

"So where'd you find the lobster?" I was torn between getting every detail and skipping to the one I really cared about.

"In the harbor," Leroy said. "Ish."

"We deduced that," I said. "Where *exactly*?"

"You mean latitude and longitude? Heck if I know."

I looked at Delphinium to see how she felt about her hero now, but her face hadn't changed.

"I could show you," Leroy said.

"In the water?" Davy said. I could feel his "no way" about to crash down like a wave. This was not his favorite kind of risk, especially since the time I'd gotten sick. He'd try pretty much anything in the digital world. He was more careful in the real one.

"You could?" I asked.

"If I wanted to," said Leroy.

"What would make you want to?"

He cocked his head to the side a little. "Respect."

Leroy was still on the top step, so I was looking up at him. That seemed a little like respect. I shut up and waited for him to speak again. That seemed like respect, too.

"Look, I never expected to find anything out there, and when I saw it—" He stopped and I thought about what it must have been like, to see something moving and real. "I thought I was saving it."

"Why didn't you call someone who could have helped?" Davy said.

"Like who?" Leroy said. "The EPF?"

"Us."

"No offense," Leroy said. "You weren't the first people I thought of. I took it back to school, and I guess I thought I might find somebody there. I ran into Derek. I knew it was over when he called his dad. Because if anyone was going to save a lobster, it was never gonna be the EPF. Right?"

"A hundred percent," I said.

"I guess that'll do," Leroy said. "For now."

I'd ridden in a canoe before. There was a fleet of them at the Mirage, a domed, man-made "lake" over on Route 22. But that canoe was nothing like the one Leroy had hidden in a pile of scrubby brush along a calm stretch of shoreline.

"I call her the *Swan*," Leroy said. "I was gonna name her after a duck, only Duckworth would have thought I was being a suck-up."

I was impressed he knew what a swan was, since that had also been declared a fragile species. Maybe there were still some out there, but I'd never seen one in real life. Ducks had not been declared a fragile species, but I'd never seen one of them in real life, either.

"It's a tree," said Davy, who usually spent so much time inside I was surprised he recognized one.

"A dugout," said Leroy. "What do you think Indigenous Americans dug out? High-grade aluminum?"

The bark had been peeled off the bottom, which was the side facing us, but you could still see the knobs where the branches used to be. It looked like it weighed a ton.

Leroy grabbed hold of it and I helped him flip it over. Now it looked more boatlike at least. He'd carved out the middle and left the sides thin, and there were two raised humps that he'd sanded into benches. I ran my hand along one of them. Smooth.

"What'd you carve it out with?" I asked him.

"I used an ax for part. And burned some of it. I was trying to be authentic. But I lasered part of it, too."

Delphinium reached out and touched the canoe. "What kind of tree was it?"

"Spruce," Leroy and I said at the same time. I was surprised he knew.

"It was already on the ground. I didn't chop it down," Leroy said. "Lightning hit it, maybe. Or it just . . . died."

"You're sure it's seaworthy?" I asked.

"It held me," he said. "Look: You want to see where I found the lobster, I'll take you. But you've got to stop questioning my handiwork."

I touched the canoe again and rocked it back and forth. It was lighter than I thought it would be. Mrs. Duckworth should have given him an A.

"Shall I get in first?" Delphinium asked.

"You can't go," Leroy said.

"Why not?" Delph looked ready for a fight.

"The *Swan* can't hold four people," Leroy said.

"I thought you said this thing was sturdy," Davy told him.

"It's a *two*-person dugout. Two benches. Two people."

"I'm underweight," I said, holding out my arms to prove it.

"I'm short," Davy added.

"Any volunteers to stay behind?" I asked.

Delph did not volunteer. Davy looked like he might, but his hand didn't go up. And it was Leroy's boat.

"Look, the four of us probably add up to two slightly overweight grown humans," I said. "It could be a test for your dugout. A buoyancy trial."

"This is at your own risk, understand?" Leroy said. "Anything happens, it's not my fault. It's not the *Swan*'s fault, either."

"Deal," I said.

"It's a great day for sailing," Delphinium said. I didn't point out that there wasn't a sail.

We hid our backpacks in the brush and lugged the canoe toward the water. Delph kept her softball mitt with her. It was kind of like a talisman, I guess.

"We split the weight," Leroy said, easing the canoe forward. "You and I each take an end. Davy and Delphinium get in the middle."

He grabbed the paddles and handed one to me. "I should make you sign something. So you don't sue."

"I wouldn't," I said.

"Swear?"

"Swear."

I crawled in first, and Leroy shoved the canoe so that my end was in the water. I dug the paddle down to the rock and sand, to hold us steady. Delphinium crawled in, keeping her hands as far from the water as possible. The boat rocked. It rocked again as Davy crawled in. Then Leroy shoved us off, the muscles on his arms bulging a little as he held tight to the sides of the canoe. He lifted his legs and swung his body over the stern, like a gymnast, avoiding the water. Then he used his paddle to propel us deeper in. We drifted until Leroy looked at me like I had the intellect of a fungus.

"What are you waiting for?" he said. "If you want to get anywhere, you've got to row."

CHAPTER 4

We angled right through murky water.

"See that island?"

I followed the invisible line that extended from Leroy's finger to a small mound in the distance. I could see some trees sticking out. It looked like one of the old harbor islands; there was nothing special about it, other than the fact that it was still there. The other islands, the ones that hadn't been washed away, barely poked out of the water. They looked like burial mounds.

"That's too far," Davy said. He believed in low expectations.

"Leroy made it out there by himself, right?" I said, wondering how he'd done it.

Leroy flexed a muscle, a joke. Still, I couldn't help but notice that he actually had a muscle to flex.

"You can't have made it there and back during study hall," I said.

"I might have skipped science," Leroy said. "And all-over fitness."

That was the one class we had together; it was so big you didn't notice if anyone was missing. The teachers never called roll.

Delphinium started chanting. "Stroke, chugga chugga. Stroke, chugga chugga. Stroke, chugga chugga," and Leroy and I worked the paddles through the water, trying to match her rhythm.

I looked for signs of an algae bloom—there was a new one off the coast, the biggest yet—but it was leagues offshore, and we were only meters. There was lots of gunk down there, which made it hard to see the bottom. The island didn't seem to be getting any closer. How *had* Leroy gone that distance alone in half a tree? That took guts.

We kept rowing. My shoulders ached, but I kept my mouth shut.

After a while, Leroy handed off his oar to Delph. I gave mine to Davy, who wrenched it through the water. "*Ex nihilo nihil fit,*" he said. "Nothing comes from nothing." He rowed some more.

Then Leroy and I took over again. Sweat dripped down my face. Delph divided her hair into three chunks and braided it down her back. She didn't have a band to hold it in place, though, so the hair parts stayed separate at the bottom, like tentacles.

The island still seemed far away. I looked back at the shore to see if anyone was watching us, but as usual, no one had ventured near the water. It was still pretty beautiful to look at, but it also smelled like the corpses of a thousand sea creatures, sort of salty and rotten.

At last I felt my paddle hit bottom again.

"We're here," Davy announced.

Leroy passed his own paddle up to Delph, who was near me at the front.

"You have to push down," he said. "The paddle's an arm. The canoe's the body. Use the arm to drag the body forward."

It was an interesting way to explain it. The two of us pressed and pulled, so the canoe's nose inched toward dry land. Leroy scooted over us and jumped out, yanking us farther up the beach. Then we all got out and helped.

"Land ho, I guess," Delphinium said.

"That's what you say when you *see* land," I told her. "There's probably something else you say when you hit it."

"Welcome," Leroy said, pounding out a drumroll on his thigh, "to my island."

The island couldn't have been much bigger than the field where Delph played softball. But it rose in a nice arc and there was a clump of trees in the middle, blocking the view of the other side; it felt bigger because we couldn't see it all.

We looked back at the shore of Blue Harbor. The sound of the highway was muffled by the surf. A lone seagull, which was not on the fragile species list because of its adaptability to eating garbage, flew overhead and cried.

"This way," Leroy said. He could have just pointed, but I let him lead us to where a stream of water rushed downhill to meet the surrounding sea.

I squatted down. "Is that fresh water?"

"I think so," Leroy said. "I haven't tasted it."

"There must be a spring somewhere in the middle. But how is that even possible? The water table—"

"See there, where they intersect?" Leroy said. "That's where I found the lobster."

"Biosphere." I occasionally used failed experiments as swear words, even though in science, failure can be a good thing; it's what leads to a breakthrough.

"Huh?" said Leroy.

"It's his idea of a swear," explained Davy.

"I told you, enough with the—"

"I'm talking about me," I said. "We should have stopped at my house to get an aquarium. And a pump. We've got nothing. Not even a bucket."

"Observe first. Act later," Delph said. She was quoting someone—maybe herself, since she was one of those people who could come up with a rule to justify whatever situation we were in. But I didn't want to act later. Later always meant "too late."

The water churned as the stream tumbled toward the ocean and the ocean pushed it back. The rocks and pebbles jumped. We stared at the spot Leroy had pointed to as if it were lit up by a cosmic spotlight, as if just talking about it would conjure the lobster back from the dead. Even without the lobster, though, there was something sort of special about that spot, about the whole island. Over the sound of the water, I heard birds—and not just sobbing seagulls, either. I saw an actual fern. If there was any place around Blue Harbor that could support life—the kind that wasn't genetically engineered in a lab or a petri dish—this could be it. It even smelled different: fresher, somehow, without the stink of decay that air fresheners could never actually freshen.

"Look," Delph whispered, pointing. "That shadow moved. Did you see it?"

"No," I admitted. "But it feels like . . . it feels like something's here."

"Very scientific, Ahab," Leroy said, squatting down to wait. I squatted, too.

If you had to guess the first person to call me Ahab instead of Jonathan, which is my given name, who would you pick?

(A) Mr. D'Angelo, my fourth-grade science teacher;

(B) Juliette, my older sister, with whom I had a textbook sibling relationship, entitling me to a lifetime supply of teasing;

(C) Derek Ripley, my sworn enemy; or

(D) Ted Goldstein, my dad.

The answer, surprisingly, is D. My dad says he started calling me Ahab, after the captain of the whaling ship in *Moby Dick*, because as a two-year-old, I showed "a startling single-mindedness" in the way I approached everything, from eating my breakfast cereal to learning the names of algae and other eukaryotic organisms. When I was older, I told him that single-mindedness in a variety of subjects wasn't single-mindedness; it was *broad*-mindedness. But the name stuck. Actually, I kind of liked it, especially when you compared it to names like Slime Boy.

"We should name this place," I said, still watching the spot where the waters met.

"It probably already has a name," said Leroy.

"I think islands have to be bigger to have names," Davy said. "This is probably something like Island Number Three. *Insula tertia*, if they're using Latin."

"Which they wouldn't be," Leroy said. "Cough. *Dead language*. Cough."

"We could name it just for us," Delphinium said. "It's a great idea."

I was glad to have a great idea attributed to me, since Leroy had spent the whole trip looking like a hero. He'd discovered the island and a lobster. Sure, he'd *killed* the lobster, but to everyone but me and maybe the EPF, that seemed to be beside the point. He'd built a boat.

"Any ideas?" I asked.

"Leroy found it," Delph said. "He should choose."

Great, I thought. *Welcome to Leroy Land*.

But Leroy just shrugged. "How about 'Bob'?" he said. "When in doubt, you should always go with 'Bob.' But if you disagree, you can call it whatever you want."

“Hope Island?” asked Delphinium.

“Except that,” Leroy said.

“Too precious,” said Davy. I secretly agreed.

“Homaridae?” I said.

“What’s that even mean?” Leroy asked.

“It’s the family name for lobster.”

“It sounds like a cheese,” Leroy said. “How about Extra Credit Island? I wouldn’t have made the boat if Duckworth wasn’t about to flunk me.”

“Look,” Delph said. “A claw.”

I leaned in closer to get a different angle on a shape hidden among the rocks. It *was* a claw. And it was attached to a lobster, a live one. It was small—about half the size of the first one Leroy had found. But unlike the lobster in the metal tank, this one was moving. I studied its shape—his shape.

“You did it!” Davy cheered like Delphinium had just discovered gold or uranium or something. Which she kind of did.

“Shh,” Leroy said as the lobster backed toward a rock. “You’ll scare it.”

“Can they even hear?” asked Delph.

“Low-frequency sounds, I think,” I told them. “But they can sense our presence. See the way he’s raising his claws?”

“How do you know it’s a he?”

“The ladies have broad, um, tails.”

“You’re kidding,” Leroy said.

“Nope. It’s for the eggs.”

"Who even *knows* this stuff?" Leroy asked.

"Ahab," Davy answered. "So now what?" He looked at me. Everybody did. But I didn't have anything to catch him with. And like Leroy said, we weren't calling Derek's dad. Just last month, the ranking officer at the EPF containment unit had been caught selling "rehabilitated specimens" to China. And he kept his job.

"Let's just watch him a minute," I said.

The wind blew. Sand stung our ankles and the sun blazed down like it was trying to melt us. Next time, we'd need more protection. I thought of my grandfather's old hip waders, which were still in the garage, near the Soov.

"He's kind of beautiful," said Delph. The lobster was, in fact, prehistoric-looking, darkish brown, with beady eyes and a tail that looked like someone had ripped it off a moth. But he was alive, and that—the alive part—made him the most beautiful thing we'd seen in months.

I blocked out everything Officer Ripley said—everything I knew—about the ocean in the twenty-first century. I took a careful step forward. The water seeped through the fabric of my shoe, warm but with a cold, sharp undercurrent.

"I just want to get a little closer," I said.

"Hold on." Delphinium went over to the canoe and grabbed her softball glove.

"It'll get wet," I said.

"That's okay."

"It might get . . ." I searched for a word to describe all the things that could happen to that glove—Polluted? Contaminated? Infected? But the stream seemed to have some sort of magic to it. Maybe Delphinium felt it, too. I put the glove over my hand. Then I picked up a piece of driftwood and placed it in the glove. I held it out to the lobster to see if he'd grab for it.

He didn't. I kept my other foot on a dry rock and started to crouch down.

EEEEERRRRRRRRRRRRRRRRR.

The noise, low and deep, came from up the hill. It didn't sound like an animal. It didn't sound human—more like an old gasoline-powered car engine, one that wasn't running right. I don't think I jumped. I don't remember anyone falling into me. But somehow I pitched sideways into the water. It wasn't just my foot that was wet now; it was all of me. Water from the stream and the harbor seeped into my pants and shirt.

I looked around, wildly. Should we find the thing making the noise? Should we *run* from the thing making the noise? I stood up, dripping, and apparently introduced a third option.

"We've got to get him home," Delph said. "Now."

She didn't mean the lobster, who had already scuttled out of sight, and she didn't mean the engine thing. She meant me.

"I'm fine," I said, standing up.

"You're not fine, Ahab." Her words were short. She sounded like she was trying not to cry.

"Delph." The water hadn't killed me that time I'd made the bet with Davy, had it?

"Just shut up," she said. "There's a reason no one goes into the harbor anymore, isn't there? A *reason*."

"The lobster looked okay."

"The lobster has adapted," Davy said. "You haven't. Remember what happened the last time? And you could already have some weird kind of flesh-eating—"

"Get in the boat," Leroy said, cutting Davy off.

"What do you think made that noise?" I said.

"Maybe it was a flesh-eating—" Davy started.

"We need to find it," I said. I meant it. I didn't just want to find the thing. I *needed* to. And okay, so maybe it would tear us to shreds before we got it in the canoe, and maybe there'd be no place to keep it if we did get it home. But I needed to see what else was alive out here.

"We'll come back," Leroy said. "After you're detoxified, or whatever. We'll bring all that equipment you mentioned. And other stuff." I could tell "other stuff" meant "weapon."

"Please?" Delph said.

It could have been all in my head, but my skin picked that moment to start itching. "Yeah, okay," I said. I handed her glove back. Water dripped from the laces. I didn't think she'd touch it, but she did, holding it away from her, between her finger and her thumb.

We got back in the boat. Since I was already wet, I stood in the water and shoved us off. As we rowed away from the island, we listened for the sound again, but all we could hear was the churning of the water and Delphinium's voice, softer and less optimistic than usual: "Stroke, chugga chugga. Stroke, chugga chugga. Stroke, chugga chugga. Stroke."

CHAPTER 5

My clothes stuck to my skin, and by the time we made it back to shore, the itch had turned into a sting. I could almost taste salt, but I tried not to lick my lips because Delphinium was right; I knew what was in the water. Garbage, chemicals, toxic algae blooms. Oil. Dye. Bleach. Paint thinner. The under-the-sink, please-dispose-of-properly containers from houses that had been swallowed by the ocean. And there were bacteria, including the flesh-eating kind that Davy had mentioned and the brain-eating kind that he hadn't.

Some of that—maybe even all of that—was on me. The second lobster seemed to be all right, but like Davy said, his body might've mutated to deal with the harbor's changes. My body had never mutated, unless zits counted as mutating. I had to get clean.

The thing is, I'd already used up my shower quota for the day. So had my parents. The only person who hadn't was Juliette, my sister, who always saved hers until Friday night, in case she had a date. She was my only hope.

I parked my bike in the garage next to the Soov, careful not to let the handlebars touch the paint. I sneaked upstairs without my mother seeing me and knocked on Juliette's bedroom door.

"Go away," she said.

"It's me."

"Like *that's* going to make a difference," she said.

"Juliette, open up. It's an emergency. Please?"

She opened the door a crack. "What do you want?"

"I need to talk to you." I stared at her right eye, which was all I could see.

Then I had to choose:

(A) Be honest. Tell her I fell in the harbor and hope that the fact that we had the same blood coursing through our veins would be enough to make her donate her shower time.

(B) Offer her money. Only, I'd spent most of my savings on parts I'd been buying to build my own CarbonClean, a water recycler that would give us all *unlimited* shower time. (Real CarbonCleans cost thousands of dollars and my dad wouldn't buy one; he was still counting on the government to miraculously end all water restrictions.)

(C) Evasive maneuvers. Ask for her shower time but don't tell her why.

(D) Jump in the shower without telling her. The alarm would go off and no water would come out when Juliette tried to use it, but sometimes it was better to apologize after you did something than to ask permission first.

I'd already knocked, though, so I started with C. "Could I borrow your shower time?"

"What? No."

"Please," I said again.

"Why?" she said. "Not that you don't *need* a shower." She wrinkled her nose, but I didn't smell too bad, at least not that I could tell.

"Because I'm your brother," I said.

"Because I'm your only brother," I added.

"Because it could be a matter of life and death," I finished.

"How is taking a shower a matter of life and death?"

So I went for A, the truth. "I sort of fell in the harbor."

"You *what*?" The door to her room opened the rest of the way. "Ahab, what were you—"

"I was trying to get something," I said. "And a wave came. It stings and I need to get whatever it is off my skin as soon as possible. Don't tell Mom."

"Thanks for that, Captain Obvious," she said. But she actually looked concerned.

"Please?" Third time's a charm. "You're the only one who can help me."

"I have a *date*."

"You won't be able to keep your date if you have to go to my funeral instead," I said. She shook her head, but I knew I'd won. "Come on, Jules." It felt like dozens of needles were poking at my skin.

"What will you give me?"

"I don't have any money."

"I'm not talking about money," she said. "I'm talking privileges. Energy points. What will you do for me?"

"I won't bug you when you go on your date." I raked my fingernails across my left arm. It didn't help. I tried slapping my arm instead.

"Not if you know what's good for you. What else?"

"I'll make your bed."

"But then you'd have to come into my room," she said. "No way."

"What do you want, then?" I gritted my teeth, not because of anger; because of the itching.

"Shower time. Not today but tomorrow—"

"It's gonna take more than one shower to get all this off me," I said.

"Then Monday," she said. "And Tuesday. I get your shower time next week."

"Deal," I said. I reached out my hand.

"I'm not touching you," she said. "But deal."

I ran to the bathroom and closed the door. If I ever did finish my own CarbonClean, I wasn't going to tell Juliette about it for at least a month.

I peeled off my pants and shirt, then my underwear. There were small welts covering my ribs and stomach. They were bright red, as if I'd been dipped in boiling water, but that could have been from the scratching. My legs seemed mostly okay. I looked down to make sure *those* parts hadn't been infected and found more spots on my inner thigh. I turned on the shower just long enough to wet my body and the soap. Then I turned the water off while I scrubbed. I soaped behind my ears and my neck and under my pits and between my toes. I shampooed my hair. I used the shampoo on my torso, too. Finally, I turned on the water and let it spray, full blast, for the last ninety glorious seconds. But the water didn't make the itchy-stingy feeling any better. It made it worse. Then the buzzer went off and the water stopped. I looked in the mirror. Spots covered nearly everywhere my clothes had been. I toweled off and used my washcloth like a pot holder to lift my wet clothes. Then I ran to my bedroom before anyone could see me.

I locked the door and grabbed my One. It was an older model, like everything else we owned, but still pretty sleek, silver and round, about the size of a river rock. I held the screen over my stomach where the spots were the worst. "Scan," I said.

Please don't let it say flesh-eating bacteria, I thought.

The One beeped, and a projection beamed onto my bedroom wall.

"Seabather's eruption," my One said. I'd set it to use the voice of Andrea Ko, an environmental activist who sounded calm yet inspirational, sort of like a superhero who does a lot of yoga. "Also known as sea lice." It was better than "flesh-eating bacteria," but Andrea's superhero voice made it sound like sea lice was an archvillain. Andrea, by the way, was rumored to be a D²—one of Darwin's Disciples.

"The skin condition known as seabather's eruption was common through the first quarter of the twenty-first century. It began in the warmer, gulf waters of Florida, and later spread through both the Pacific and Atlantic, with cases reported as far north as Maine and into Canada. The lice, also known as thimble jellyfish, are difficult to see with the naked eye. The result, however, is easy to see, in red lesions that cover the body, particularly in the areas where swimsuits or clothing are worn. The rash went into a decline as ocean sport and sea bathing lost popularity, but the severity of each case increased, as did allergic reactions. Symptoms accompanying the eruption can but do not always include: itching, nausea, vomiting, diarrhea, malaise, headache, muscle spasms, depression, swelling, and, in rare cases, death."

Andrea Ko sounded almost cheery when she said "death."

Nausea. Yeah, I was feeling that. I hoped I could avoid everything else, especially the death part. I ran another search to come up with the cure, which boiled down to prescription medication, which I couldn't get without my parents knowing. Other suggestions included time, rest, and black salve. We had some of that. My mother put black salve on everything. There were tubes in the bathroom, in the junk drawer in the kitchen, in the glove compartment of

CHAPTER 6

"Nice to see you, Peter," my mother was saying. "Oh, and here's Jonathan. I believe he's in your brother's grade, isn't he? Jonathan, do you know Peter?"

"Yes." I used as few syllables as possible.

"Hi, *Jonathan*," Peter said. "It's so wonderful to see you."

My skin was already crawling, but with Peter in the house, it was worse. He smiled so I could see all his teeth, which were perfect, of course. My mom and Juliette had to know he wasn't being sincere. I mean, who talks like that?

Everybody in Blue Harbor—with the possible exception of my sister and my mother—knew Peter Ripley was a jerk. Delphinium said every time she went to the bathroom during a Blue Harbor football game, there was some girl in there crying over something he'd said or done—or said he'd done in those rare instances when he hadn't done anything at all. Juliette and I didn't always get along, but she was my sister. Peter was a cockroach.

Juliette smiled and adjusted the strap on her sundress. It was blue, and her shoulders sparkled with this shimmer stuff she used sometimes. Her hair was dark and curly like mine, but long, so it grew down instead of out.

"Shouldn't she have a sweater?" I said "sweater" but I was thinking "armor" or "hazmat suit." I looked at my dad, who was whacking the refrigerator to get it to stop buzzing.

"Since when are you my wardrobe consultant?" Juliette asked.

"I think she looks lovely," Peter said.

I tried my mother. "What about the elements?" The word hung heavy in the air.

"I'm wearing lotion," Juliette said. "And the sun's going down."

"Studies show that lotion alone—"

"Oh, bring a sweater, just to humor him," said my mother.

"I'll roast," Juliette said. "I'll roast and melt." But she ran upstairs to get a sweater. "You promised not to mess this up," she hissed as she walked past me.

"You'll have her home on time?" my father said to Peter. "Otherwise, I might have to call the police. Oh, wait." He winked. "That's your dad, isn't it?"

Peter laughed, like my father was actually funny. "You don't have to worry about me, sir."

I didn't say anything as Juliette ran back downstairs carrying a sweater, grabbed Peter by the hand again, and yanked him out the door, as if exposing him to us was the thing that was dangerous. The door slammed shut behind them.

"Well," my mother said. "What a nice boy."

"That was Peter *Ripley*," I said. "He's a jerk. He's scum. He's . . ."

"He's Angus Ripley's son," my father said. His voice had a trace of a growl. "Well. If things work out, maybe Angus will do something about those green slips."

"It won't work out," I said. *You're the one who needs to do something about the green slips*, I thought. "Peter Ripley has dated about a million girls."

"Your sister is one in a million," my mother said, trying to put a positive spin on it. It was like there was some kind of autocorrect in her brain.

"He never stays with any girl for more than a couple of weeks," I said.

"Then we'll have to hope he fixes those tickets early," my dad said.

"Ted."

"I'm joking," my father said. "Can't you tell when I'm joking?" He looked over at me. "Ahab's joking, too."

"No," I told him. "I'm not."

"Well, you know the old saying," my mother said. "'If you can't say anything nice . . .'" My mother was like all three of those little monkeys, the ones with their hands over their ears and eyes and mouths. She was a news photographer a long time ago, but when Juliette was born, she switched to shooting products instead. Her job was to make things look better than they were. I guess that extended to real life, too. If she'd taken a photo of Peter Ripley, she would have labeled it CHARMING BOY WITH LOTS OF POTENTIAL. There would have been nothing about his dating record or the fact that he'd been making out with Helene Weaver in front of the convenience store where everyone could see.

"Dinner's on the table," my mother said. "Sit."

I sat and sneaked a scratch on my arm when she wasn't looking. We were having ficken again—a protein substitute that was shaped like drumsticks.

"Why do they do that?" I asked.

"Do what, dear?"

"It would taste better if it wasn't pretending to be something else," I said.

"Your grandmother made the best fried chicken," my dad said. "We'd be on our bikes, two blocks, three blocks away, and we could smell it cooking."

I reached into a bowl and snagged a vegibar. My father grabbed a vegibar, too, and I leaned my head against my shoulder to block out the sound of his chewing.

"How was residency?" my mother asked. That's what we called the school semesters we attended in person. Other semesters we attended remotely, to help alleviate overcrowding, but she never asked, "How was remotely?"

"The usual." I rubbed my back against the slats on my chair.

"Are you breaking out? Here, let me look."

"I'm fine," I said.

"Put something on it," she said. "Some salve. I hope it wasn't a mosquito."

"Mosquitoes," my father said. "When I was a kid—"

"Did Grandma fry those, too?" I asked.

"Ha-ha. Very funny. No, she didn't fry them. She swatted them. They were different than the ones you see today. Bigger. Real bloodsuckers. When I took my bike trip to Canada . . ."

My father's bike trip to Canada was a favorite topic of conversation. Correction: monologue. For a conversation, someone else has to talk, too.

I knew the particulars. The border wasn't far away, and he and his friends made it in three days, camping at night and watching meteor showers. "My friend Tim got a mosquito bite near his upper lip," my father said. "Made his whole mouth look like he'd been in a boxing ring. Those mosquitoes were the size of dragonflies. Heck. They were the size of birds."

I'd seen photos of my father's bike, blue, with handlebars that curved in a spiral, like the inside of a seashell. It didn't look so different from my own bike. You'd think they would have upgraded the technology or replaced bikes with space skates or something. But when you have a perfect design, I guess you don't mess with it.

"You must have spent too much time outside," my mother told me. "It's nothing to make light of, Jon. Look at your face!"

I touched my hands to my face. Had the eruptions spread? But she was just talking about sunburn.

"You've got to be more careful. Did you even have a hat?"

"Forgot it," I said.

"Tomorrow's Saturday. That's a beautiful day to be inside. Why don't you go to the lake? There's a new one over on Buoy."

The new lake, Utopia, was in one of the giant warehouses on the south side of town. Places like these were called Rec Boxes™ and were known for "bringing the outside in!" Their other slogan, "It's a beautiful day to be inside," had been around so long, I wasn't even sure my mother knew she was quoting a commercial. They were nice enough, but you could hear the currents of the air vents. They tried to cover it up with nature sounds. And there were places where the dirt and sand had worn away and you could see cement flooring underneath.

My dad used to take me fishing at the Rec Boxes™ when I was little, or on hikes. Besides lakes, there were Rec Box™ forests with labyrinths of walking trails. They had cheesy names like Eden and Eden II and the Mirage, where I'd gone canoeing. They had no mosquitoes.

"Yeah, okay," I told my mom. "Maybe I'll check it out." But there was only one place I wanted to spend my Saturday, and that was on Leroy's island, searching for whatever had made the errr sound. If I could discover what made it, I might be able to contribute something real to the world of science. Something real and big. Something that the Disciples would notice.

My One beeped and a projection of Delphinium's head rose out of it.

"Hi, Delphinium," my mother said. "We're in the middle of dinner. Jonathan, you know you're not supposed to have that at the table."

"Sorry, Mrs. Goldstein," Delph called. "Holler back when you're done, Ahab." Her face disappeared again.

"You know what I heard today?" my father said. He worked in network repair, usually from home, but he still somehow absorbed local gossip. "You'll like this, Ahab. I heard that some kid at your school found a lobster. A live one."

"I heard that, too," I said.

"Maybe they're making a comeback. You should have seen the lobsters we caught when I was a kid. We'd eat the meat on hot dog buns. At the Lobster Pool, remember, Mon?"

"Of course I remember," my mother said. Her first name was Monica, but my dad never used the whole thing.

"We caught them in traps, those lobsters. Mr. Stinson paid us twenty dollars to go around and check them. You wouldn't believe the claws. Remember that, Mon? Remember the size of those claws?"

"I remember," my mother said. Her voice was softer this time. "I remember."

CHAPTER 7

I tried to get comfortable before I called Delph. Lying down stung—as if my bed was made of broken glass. Sitting up didn't help—my shirt seemed to be made of broken glass, too. Taking off my shirt *might* have helped, but I didn't want Delph to see my chest until I'd had a chance to do more push-ups. Also until I was less rashy.

"Delphinium," I said. "Interface." The One made the connection and her head appeared in a beam of light, just above my dresser.

"Are you okay?" she asked, without saying hello.

"Define 'okay.'"

"Are you puking?" she said. "Is your skin green? Are chunks of your flesh rotting and falling off? Do you feel like you're dying?"

"My skin is not green," I said. "I do not feel like I'm dying."

"You didn't answer the puking or rotting flesh part."

"Astute," I said.

"You still didn't answer. Come on. I live for this stuff." Delphinium wanted to be a doctor—the research kind, not the stick-out-your-tongue kind. Still, diseases fascinated her.

I breathed through my nose for a few seconds, to let whatever was rising in my throat fall back again. "I haven't puked," I said. "But not because I haven't felt like it. I have a rashy thing, but I don't think my skin is actually rotting."

"What kind of a rashy thing?"

"A rashy thing," I said. "Bumps and stuff. You don't want the details."

"But I do. Show me."

"It'll be gone by tomorrow."

"You'll show me tomorrow?"

"Yeah, no," I said. "'Come see my rash.' That's not the world's greatest line."

"Are you giving me a line?"

Wait a minute. Was this:

(A) flirting,

(B) teasing,

(C) banter, or

(D) the regular sort of conversation you'd have with a friend?

It could have been D, though there might have been a hint of A, at least on my part, not that I was experienced with A. But my gut said it was probably C. Delphinium was good at C. That's the thing about multiple-choice questions. On school tests, there was always more than one plausible answer, but there was only one *best* answer. The multiple-choice tests cut down on teachers' workloads, but they didn't allow you to show reasoning, so there was no partial credit. Soon, someone will probably invent a scanner that will read whether the right answer is in your brain or not. Maybe an invention like that would give partial credit. That inventor won't be me, though. Technology like that would lead to too many embarrassing situations. Plus espionage.

"You'd tell me if it was something really bad, wouldn't you? Like if you were dying or if you had a renegade amoeba up your nose."

If I had a band, which would require playing an instrument, I would call it Renegade Amoeba. "I would tell you," I said.

"Good."

"Have you talked to anyone else?" I asked. What I meant was: Had she talked to Leroy?

"Nobody else fell in."

"I want to go back," I told her.

"We will."

"Tomorrow," I added.

"We can't tomorrow," Delphinium said.

"Why not?" What if the Errr thing escaped? Or died before we discovered it? What if the EPF got there first?

"Because you're sick," she said.

"So?" I said. Captain Ahab wouldn't have let a rash keep him from going after Moby Dick.

"And anyway, you haven't checked it out with Leroy."

"How do you know I haven't talked to him?"

"What do you mean?"

"I mean, how do you know I didn't talk to Leroy? Maybe I've been talking to him all night. Maybe he came over for dinner and he's downstairs talking to my parents right now. The only way you'd know I haven't talked to him is if *you* talked to Leroy and he said I hadn't talked to him."

"Do you have sun-brain?" she said. "Or maybe you have one of those brain-eating—"

"Aha!" I said.

"Ahab, seriously. I didn't talk to Leroy. And the reason I assumed you didn't talk to Leroy is because I'm not sure you even *like* Leroy."

"Do you?"

"Do I what?"

"Like Leroy?"

"Of course I like him. What I don't know is why *you* don't like him."

"I like him fine," I said.

"You could have fooled me."

"I guess I did," I said. "Ha."

"Ahab?"

"What?"

"You should go to bed."

"You sound like my mother," I said.

"I don't know who you sound like," she said. "But you don't sound like you."

I didn't feel like me, either. I wondered if brains could itch, because I felt like my whole body was crawling, not just my brain and skin but my liver and my kidneys, too. "I'm calling Leroy right now," I said. "To ask about tomorrow."

"Bye," she said.

"And I'm not sick," I said. "It's just a rashy thing." But her projection had already faded.

"Find Leroy Varney, Blue Harbor," I told my One. "Interface."

Leroy's face filled the beam that Delphinium had abandoned.

"Are you okay?" he said. He obviously didn't want to be responsible for two deaths—mine and the lobster's—in the same day.

"When can we go back?" I asked.

"Sunday, maybe," he said. "If you aren't contaminated."

"Why not tomorrow?"

"I'm going with my dad to New Arcadia tomorrow," he said.

"Maybe we can borrow—"

"The *Swan* doesn't go out without the captain."

I could have sneaked down there and taken the boat, since I knew he'd be occupied. But I wasn't a thief. And to tell the truth, I wasn't sure I could handle it by myself. To find the Errr thing, I'd need some backup. Besides, I didn't want to prove Delphinium right by being a total jerk.

"Okay, Sunday," I said.

"Feel better."

"I'm fine." But when he was gone, I scratched my back against my bedpost before trying Delphinium again.

"Sorry I was weird," I said. I hoped my appearance of general discomfort would make her accept my apology.

"You're always a *little* weird."

"Thanks." Pause. "Leroy says we can go back on Sunday."

"Good. You should rest tomorrow."

"My mom says I should go to a lake."

"It's a beautiful day to be inside," she said.

"Do you want to come?"

"Which one are you going to?"

"Utopia," I said. I was close enough to her projection to see that her lips were a little chapped. "It's new."

"Yeah, I'll go. Why not? Did you ask Davy?"

"I think he has something with his mom." This wasn't a total lie. Davy almost always had something with his mom. It wasn't like I meant it to be a date or anything; Delphinium and I were just friends. It was just that sometimes it felt like we could be more. Even if we couldn't, it was nice to hang out just us two. I twitched and started to scratch again but pulled my hand back at the last minute.

"You should let me see that rash," she said. "I'm getting really good at skin things. I've been practicing."

"I'm fine," I said, wondering how you could practice something like that.

"Are not. See you tomorrow."

"Am so. Okay."

As soon as her face dissolved, I started scratching.

CHAPTER 8

I met Delphinium at the Utopia at ten. The advertisement had promised *"cutting-edge plant life and authentic EnviroSounds packaged together to create an unbeatable outdoor experience. Step inside and go outdoors!"* We went to the ticket counter, wondering what kind of plant life was considered "cutting edge."

"Members?" asked the woman. She was youngish and professional-looking, with a high-collared shirt and perfect hair. She was also glowing, which, combined with a certain wispy quality, made it clear she was a hologram.

"No, not members," I said.

"That will cost you thirty-five dollars apiece. Together or separate?"

"Together," I said. Even though it wasn't a date, I held out my index finger.

"Separate," Delphinium said, holding out her own.

I held my finger up to the scanner and waited for the red light to change to green. Then Delph waved her finger in the same spot.

We thought about renting a boat, for practice, but Delphinium pointed out that it didn't exactly mimic real conditions for the *Swan*. My shoulders still hurt, so I didn't argue with her.

"Fishing license?" the woman asked.

"No," I said. "I don't believe in fishing just for the halibut." The hologram lady completely missed my pun, which I thought was pretty good, considering how many fish were considered fragile species.

"We don't even need to mullet over," said Delphinium.

"Impressive," I said.

"I've been studying up," said Delph.

"Have a nice day," said the woman.

Delph and I entered a tunnel, which was decorated with ivy. Inside, it was dark, like a cave, which made the brightness seem brighter when the tunnel ended and we entered Utopia.

The room was about 180 meters long, most of it taken up by a small lake, which was pierced, now and then, with pillars, decorated to look like trees. There was a domed ceiling, onto which a sky was projected. The clouds actually moved, which already made it more authentic than Eden II. A narrow beach bordered the lake with clean white sand. A family had a blanket spread on top of it, and two boys were building castles, then smashing them.

Surrounding the lake was a wooded area with a trail. The whole place smelled like a combination of plants, plastic, mold, new carpeting, and something that could have been chlorine but probably wasn't, since that wouldn't be good for the fish. The lake was a rich blue color. Morning glories—real ones, I think—wound around the fake trees. It was peaceful, but it didn't make me feel peaceful; it just made me want to get back to Leroy's island. Maybe the Errr thing was the key to saving the world.

"It's beautiful," Delphinium said. "Mostly."

I didn't need a brain scanner to know she was giving only partial credit, because it was only partially real.

We could see movement in the lake. Canoes, more professional-looking than Leroy's, went back and forth along the water. Circles of ripples dotted the surface. A sign on the bank said: CATCH AND RELEASE ONLY. And then, in smaller letters: UTOPIA IS NOT RESPONSIBLE FOR ANY ILLNESS ASSOCIATED WITH THE EXPOSURE TO OUR "WILDLIFE."

A high-pitched, pulsing sound seemed to come from the walls. Crickets? I spotted a speaker in one of the trees, covered with ivy, and another on the ground, inside a fake rock. A moment later, the sound changed from crickets to the chirping of birds. Then there was a roar.

"Is that supposed to be a tiger?" Delphinium asked.

"The famous lake tiger, indigenous to . . . no North American lake ever. Very vicious," I said.

"Grrrr," she said. "Come on. Let's walk." Delph stepped onto the trail, which was big enough for both of us to walk side by side, unless we passed someone coming from the other direction. I pretended the breeze wasn't being generated by an HVAC system.

"So," Delph said. "When do I get to see the rash?"

"That would be never," I said.

"Did you go to the doctor?"

"Nope."

"Not even a Screen Doc?" Screen Doctors were available via the One on a twenty-four-hour basis. But I knew the diagnosis.

"Can't we talk about something else?" I asked.

"You mean something *besides* your intriguing and potentially embarrassing physical ailments?" Delph said. "Let's not make any *rash* decisions."

"Delphinium."

"This is turning into a bumpy conversation," she said.

The thing about Delphinium is: She's funny. And smart and athletic and all that. She could hang out with anyone. But here she was at Utopia on a Saturday morning—with me.

"How's your glove?" I asked, changing the subject and showing that I cared about her personal possessions at the same time.

"I washed it," she said, "which apparently you're not supposed to do with real leather. But then I put some restore stuff on it that my grandfather had under the sink. Maybe it'll work."

"You might try some heat, too. Air drying might not kill the—"

"Flesh-eating bacteria?"

"Jellyfish," I said. "I'm pretty sure I was attacked by thimble jellyfish."

"Is that what you have all over you? Stings?"

She pulled out her One and held it to her lips. "Identify: thimble jellyfish," she said.

A second later, the description beamed out in front of us. Mercifully, she had turned off the sound, so I didn't have to hear a stranger's voice say with athletic jocularity, "Also known as sea lice." I did have to hear Delphinium say it, though.

"You have LICE?"

"Shhh," I said. "And it's *sea* lice. It's another name for jellyfish larvae. That's what makes the rash."

"That's what makes it disgusting," she said.

"Is that how you're going to talk to your patients?"

"I'm going to be in a lab. Does it hurt?" she asked.

"It stings," I admitted. "And it itches a lot. But it'll be gone in a week."

"And you still want to go back?"

"It's not like we're going to swim," I said. "But yes. Of course. Don't you?"

"Sure. But there's no rush," she said.

I looked around at all the fake trees. "Yes," I said. "There is."

Delphinium got my drift, which is one of the things I like about her. We stopped under a tree, a real one this time, covered in delicate white blossoms. When the wind came, which it did about once every eight minutes, they fell like snow. Delphinium reached out her hand to catch some.

"It's a Bradford pear," I said. "They grow fast, but they don't live long. Not a prime choice for the green canopy."

"They're in a warehouse," she said. "They don't *have* to contribute to the green canopy."

"In the real world, you wouldn't even have Bradford pears growing near a lake," I said. "You'd have—"

"Don't pick it apart," she said.

"You're the one who pointed out the tiger," I said.

"The tiger was *obvious*."

"Tra-la-la," I said, channeling my mother's ability to ignore anything that didn't fit into her desired worldview. "What a beautiful day for a walk."

"Better," she said, patting me on my shoulder.

"OW." My skin burned when she touched it. "Easy."

"Sorry."

We walked a little more.

EEEERRRRRRRRRRRRRRRRRR.

And froze. It wasn't a tiger; it was a sound, *the* sound, the same sound we'd heard on the island. It seemed familiar, and not because we'd heard it just yesterday. I recognized it from someplace else. A movie? From school? I started searching the bushes before I remembered that it was just a recording. I held up my One to see if it could identify the sound, but I was too slow.

"Come on." I grabbed Delph's arm and pulled her back up the path.

"It's just a soundtrack," she said.

"I know," I said. "But maybe there's a credit list. Chirp of the Sparrow. Roar of the Tiger. Errr of the . . . Whatever." I didn't believe in fate, except the kind created by cause and effect. But I believed in coincidences, and this was a big one. We went back to the lady at the desk.

"I hope you've enjoyed your stay. I'm sorry, there are no refunds." Her voice had a weird, echoing quality.

"We don't want a refund," I said. "We want to know the name of the soundtrack you play—the one with the nature sounds."

"You want to know the name of the soundtrack we play, the one with the nature sounds?" She repeated exactly what I said, only she made it sound like a question.

"We just really like nature," Delphinium said. "We were thinking it would be fun to get the music—the sounds—to play at home. Is it for sale? Could you tell us who makes it?"

"Each Rec Box soundtrack is specially made to bring you, the customer, an authentic experience with maximum enjoyment potential. Our soundtracks are not shared outside the Rec Box experience."

"Look," Delphinium said, in the reasonable voice she uses with teachers and parents. "We're not going to open our own Rec Box. We're just two nature-deprived kids who want to hear some nature sounds in the comfort of our own homes. Could you at least tell us the name of the recording?"

"Could I tell you the name of the recording?" the woman repeated.

"Yes," I said.

"No," she said.

I changed directions. "What about the animals?" I said. "Could you tell us the animals that appear on Utopia's nature soundtrack?"

"Yes, I can tell you the animals that appear on Utopia's nature soundtrack," she said.

"Great," I said.

"Yes," she agreed. "It *is* great. The animals that are on Utopia's nature soundtrack are lake animals."

Delphinium thanked her, laughing a little. I didn't thank her. I didn't laugh, either. We walked back toward the lake, just in time to hear the eee-eee of a dolphin, which I recognized, and a screeching sound I didn't recognize at all.

I tried to mimic the errr sound for my One, hoping the recognition software could get me in the ballpark. "Errrrrr," I said.

"Cow, sick," the One responded.

"I don't think there's a 'cow, sick' on the island," I said. But that introduced a new possibility. What if the thing we heard on the island was sick? I was pretty sure discovering another sick and dying animal wouldn't make me a D^2. But what if I could save it?

"Whatever it is, we'll find out tomorrow," Delphinium said.

One thing we knew for sure: Whatever made that sound was not a lobster.

CHAPTER 9

It was eight a.m. and the sun was already blazing. We'd brought hats, the kind with little curtains to protect our necks. Delph had an umbrella.

"It's in case anyone watching wants to turn us into a painting," she said. I didn't think anyone would want to paint a bunch of geeky kids rowing a tree across the harbor. And I hoped nobody would be watching.

We loaded Leroy's canoe with gloves, tongs, test tubes, tweezers, an eyedropper, a net, a rope, snacks, and my grandfather's hip waders. Leroy had brought a lead pipe—his weapon of choice, I guess. I'd also brought my science bag, an aquarium, an air pump, and Davy's dog kennel, which was too small for a tiger but could accommodate a raccoon.

"My mom will kill me if she finds out," he said. "Obliterate. *Extirpate.*"

"She won't find out," Delph said.

Leroy smiled. I had a feeling that the list of things his own parents didn't find out was pretty long.

Rowing was easier this time, the rhythm in our heads without Delph having to call it out. Instead, she threw out more potential names for the island.

"Leahdelvy? It's the first part of all our first names." She'd put Leroy's first, of course. I concentrated on rowing. The sweat made my rash itch worse, even though I'd slathered on black salve. To hide the rash from my friends and the sun, I'd also put on long sleeves, so my arms and body felt like the inside of a sandwich. The salve was the mustard.

"What first?" Leroy asked as we dragged the canoe ashore. He was captain, but he seemed willing to take orders.

I wanted to run straight up the hill, but we needed to be methodical. Besides, we might find a lobster. "We should start at that spot," I said. "Where the waters meet."

I was wearing my grandfather's hip waders, so I crossed to the other side of the stream. I crouched and waited. The sound of the water lapping at the shore blocked out my nervous breathing, and made our silence seem not so awkward.

After a few minutes of nothing happening, Delphinium picked up a black rock, smaller than a baseball but almost as round. She tossed it and caught it, tossed it and caught it. Leroy picked up a rock, too, flattish, slate, and sent it skipping into the water. It bounced three times before it sank. Davy tried to skip one. If it was a virtual rock, it wouldn't have been a problem for him. But it was real, so it was.

"You need to angle it at about twenty degrees," I told him. I was about to mention hydrodynamics when Leroy picked up another rock and handed it to him.

"Put your finger here," he said. "Nope. Yeah. Okay. Try again."

"Just aim it in that direction," I said. "So you don't scare anything away." I looked back at the water.

Davy threw another rock.

"You have to spin it a little," Leroy said. "Here." I looked up, just in time to see it skip.

"You see that?" Davy said. "You see that?!"

Leroy grinned. "Flick the next one harder. It might go twice."

Davy kept flicking. I kept scanning the water. Nothing moved, so I studied the island. From a distance, it had looked like a circle, except for one part, where it jutted into the water in a point. From above, it must have looked like a lumpy, tree-covered teardrop. The errr sound had felt like it was everywhere at once, amplified somehow, but I had a feeling the root of it was somewhere in the trees. "Let's go," I said. "We can look for the lobster later."

We each grabbed something for the trek uphill. I noticed Leroy grabbed the pipe. I grabbed a net and a pocketful of test tubes.

We followed the stream. The incline was steep. If you had short legs, like Davy, it probably felt like mountain climbing. But he kept up all the way to the top, where we found a small, clear pool that spilled down the hill like lava. Behind it were two large rocks with a space between them that looked almost like the mouth of a cave.

"Ponce de León, eat your heart out," Delphinium said. Her voice echoed, amplified. You could tell how tense the moment was, because nobody checked their One to look up Ponce de León. (For the record, he was an explorer who searched for the Fountain of Youth and found Florida instead.)

Whatever made the errr sound had probably stood exactly where Delphinium was standing. But no one was here now.

She stepped to the side. "Hello?" she said. This time, her voice was normal.

The spring was easy to spot: a bubbling, churning spot where the water couldn't sit still. I reached out and touched the water—without gloves. I cupped my hand and held some.

"I don't know about that," Davy muttered. He moved into the echo zone. "I don't know, bruh," he said, louder. And then in Latin: "I don't know, frater."

"But look at it," I said, letting the water drip back into the pool. It was clear as glass. You could see every rock on the bottom.

"The water looked nice at the Utopia, too," Delph pointed out.

But this was different. The water had a crisp quality to

it; it didn't feel soft like the water at home. I opened one of my test tubes, filled it, and stoppered the top. Then I filled another, in case the first tube broke.

Leroy didn't say a word about my playing scientist, which is what Derek Ripley would have done. *Look at Slime Boy. What a poser.*

I flipped over a rock, hoping something underneath it would scurry out. Nothing. Davy and Delph each put on a pair of gloves and started flipping rocks, too. So did Leroy, without gloves. I don't know if it was because he trusted me, or because he wanted to show that if I wasn't afraid, he wasn't, either. Each time he grabbed a rock, he flung it down the hill, crackling through the trees.

"You'll mess up the ecosystem," I said. "And you might hit something."

"Like what?"

ERRRRRR. The noise came right on cue, strong and loud.

We froze, all except Leroy, who reached for his pipe again. I got that feeling in my legs, like electricity. I grabbed my net and moved to the end of the pool, the side farthest from the lava stream.

Leroy and Delph followed me. We moved quietly and hoped the ERRR thing wouldn't run. But part of me thought the thing wasn't scared of us. It must have seen us; that's why it called out.

I heard the buzz of a cicada, a real one. And from below, I could still hear the ocean. It sounded a lot like the nature soundtrack at the Utopia. The only thing missing was the tiger.

ERRRR.

The sound came from someplace low, near the ground.

I squatted low, too.

EEERRRR. RUP.

There: a pair of eyes protruding from the water. They were yellow, with black specks, like bugs in amber. The black pupil wasn't round but more like a flattened football. The rest of it was covered in water, but I could make out a squat body and long, folded legs. It was a frog. A monster of a frog, the likes of which I hadn't seen—well, okay. Ever.

The noise had sounded like it had come from something bigger, but this must have been what made it. A frog.

When the fragile species list (formerly known as the endangered species list) had its growth spurt, frogs were the first thing on it. It had something to do with their immunity, fungus, and the changes in temperature that affected their breeding habits. I'd read about it for a report I did for science class, which wasn't about frogs, or even amphibians, but about the fragile list in general. The Panamanian golden frog went first, a part of the old list, along with the Wyoming toad and the mountain chicken frog. They'd started as endangered, then they went extinct. More common frogs went next. Wood frogs. Spring peepers. Until they were almost all gone.

"How did that little thing make so much noise?" Delph whispered behind me.

"He's not so little," I whispered back. "Look at him. He's a monster."

Slowly, slowly, I raised my net.

Then I lowered it down and—yes! I had just caught what was, beyond a doubt, the last frog in Blue Harbor, Maine.

CHAPTER 10

"Nice catch," said Delphinium, though it wasn't like the frog had tried to escape.

"I just want to see it a little closer," I said. "For now." We'd caught a frog. A frog! No one had seen one in years. Would just catching one make me eligible to be a Disciple?

"What kind is it?" Leroy asked, drumming his hands on his leg.

"The rare kind," Davy said. "Even more rare than your lobster."

"It's a bullfrog," I said. "It has to be. They're supposedly the only ones left." The bullfrogs had been on the fragile species list for years, but they hadn't passed over to extinct. They were stronger than the other frogs, and pretty much the only frogs in Maine that hadn't been wiped out by a combination of pesticides, fungus, pollution, disease, loss of habitat, and climate change. They were the Hercules of frogs. But no one had seen one—in captivity or out—in a very long time. The government had made it harder to declare things extinct, but that was probably the only reason the bullfrog hadn't been. Well, that and the fact that we were staring one in the face.

"At least it's not a tiger," said Delph.

"Tiger?" The hitch in Davy's voice told me that he was afraid the frog wasn't the only living thing on the island. I was afraid that it was.

"Inside joke," Delph said.

"I've never seen one, not even in the tanks," Leroy said. "That is one weird-looking critter."

When my dad was in high school, they dissected frogs in biology, virtually, anyway. In my science class, we were preparing to dissect virtual worms. Frogs weren't in the curriculum. Why bother dissecting something that didn't exist?

"I don't get it," Delphinium said. "How could it survive? It's not that different here, is it? I mean from there?" She pointed across the water, at Blue Harbor.

"It's cool, right?" Leroy said. The "right" gave him ownership. The "right" said, "I was on this island first." He was a little farther away from the rocks, so his voice wasn't amplified as much. Then he said, "I mean cool, temperature-wise. It feels cooler than on the mainland. Maybe that's the difference."

He was right: The air did feel cooler.

But that could have been for a lot of reasons:

(A) It really was cooler.

(B) Leroy was an expert in the power of suggestion.

(C) The frog was cold-blooded, and I was having some sort of empathy mind-meld thing.

Cold-blooded didn't really mean the frog's blood was cold, by the way. It just meant his temperature depended on the environment surrounding him, which in this case was the spring.

"So now what?" Leroy said.

The frog answered first. His throat filled with air. He looked like he was getting ready to hurl. Then he let out that sound again. EEERRRRRR.

This time, it sounded less like a tiger or scraping furniture or even cow, sick. It sounded kind of sad.

I started giving orders.

"Delph: Go get the aquarium. Leroy: Get some rocks and stuff and make a habitat. Wear gloves. Davy: Hold the net."

I pulled out my One and started snapping photos: Close. Far away. The habitat. Leroy, standing in the background and holding up the peace sign. The frog, close-up again. I switched to X-ray mode to take a shot of its internal organs. I switched modes again. The next time it talked, I searched for an exact identification. It didn't say, "Cow, sick," this time. It said, "Bullfrog, American."

The frog must be male, because females, according to the entry, didn't usually vocalize. The One told us, in Andrea Ko's superhero voice, that males do, loudly, to attract the ladies and to stake out their territory. They live—or lived—near ponds and lakes. Our spring wasn't either, but at least that line proved that the hologram's answer ("lake animals") wasn't totally wrong. Tigers loved the water, too, it turned out, so maybe she wasn't completely wrong about that, either, just about the country they inhabited. Or used to.

When frogs were full size, like our frog, they ate snakes and mice and fish.

Maybe that was why we hadn't seen any other small creatures on the island; maybe the frog had eaten them.

Delph came back with the aquarium and we set it up with water and the rocks and plants that Leroy had gathered.

I slid on my gloves—more to protect the frog than to protect myself. He was heavy and slimy when I lifted him. He didn't complain, just settled into a corner of the tank and waited. I put a screen over the top.

"Do we report it?" Davy asked. He usually preferred to stay below the radar.

"How do you say 'heck, no' in Latin?" asked Leroy.

"I was just checking," Davy said.

"We're not reporting it," I repeated. The new government wasn't protecting the environment any more than the old one was. They'd admitted there was a problem, which was good. But they were just pretending to help. Davy knew that. He was an expert at figuring out which government-released images were real and which were fakes. The ones of President Franco standing next to restored swampland or a baby cheetah? Propaganda. Also: totally bogus.

"Then what are we doing?" Davy asked.

"Gathering information. Our own information."

The frog croaked again and Leroy jumped back and forth between two rocks, a sort of victory dance.

"The next thing we should do," I said, "is see if there are any more."

We fanned out. Leroy went down the hill, to where he'd found the first lobster, with Davy as his partner. Delphinium and I searched around the spring. The frog called out again from the aquarium, but no one called back.

"Poor thing," Delphinium said. "If he has a girlfriend, she's not speaking to him."

"I don't think she would anyway," I said. "The females don't talk."

"Well, that's oppressive," Delph said. "Wait. If the females don't talk, how do we know there *isn't* a female out there somewhere? If we take him, he could be leaving behind a girlfriend. *We'd never know.*"

Delphinium had a point. If we took the frog away, we were taking away his chance to find a mate. Plus, he could die. I thought about the way Leroy's lobster had looked in the EPF tank with the tail curled under.

My aquarium, with a water pump, was better than Leroy's bucket. But what if it wasn't enough? A dead frog wasn't going to get me into the Disciples. It might even get me banned. For life.

"Maybe we could leave him here for a while," I said. "But we could tag him. And watch him."

"And his girlfriend," said Delphinium.

"If he has one," I said.

We searched a while longer but still didn't find much wildlife, besides the usual insects. We found plants, though, that I hadn't seen on the mainland. Mayapple, according to the One, and something else it identified as winterberry. We heard birds, camouflaged in the trees. What if one of them tried to eat my frog? Our frog. Still, he'd made it this long.

Davy and Leroy made it back up the hill, and I outlined my new plan.

"You always carry a tag in your pocket?" Leroy said.

"No," I said. "Just today." I dug into my bag and pulled out a small vial full of microchips, each less than a centimeter long. I'd bought them years ago, but I had yet to inject them under the skin of any actual animals. The closest I'd come was Davy's shoe, plus a cockroach that I'd tracked through our house for a week before my dad stomped on him.

"Will it hurt him?" Delph asked.

"No. Not if I do it right." *Could* I do it right?

"Just don't plug him in the heart or the eyeball," Leroy advised.

"Thanks." I knew I wouldn't hit a heart or an eyeball, but an artery was a possibility. My hand shook, and all I was doing was holding the chip, not even inserting it.

Davy pulled out his own One, which read aloud (in the voice of British gamer Rudy Janowitz) a story about a group of scientists who had tagged frogs back in the 1930s. They'd put metal tags around the dentary bone. "Which would be here," Davy said, pointing to his jaw. "Delph could do it. She has steady hands."

Delphinium shook her head. "If that's really the last bullfrog, I'm not going to be responsible for killing him. No way."

"Maybe we can just use this," said Leroy. He held up a tube of Bind-oh. "I've had it on my skin tons and it hasn't hurt me."

"That'll work," Davy said.

"It seems safer than breaking the skin," Leroy said.

"It does," said Delph.

It did. Maybe if I'd practiced more, or even done one of those virtual dissections, it would have been different. But the frog was so delicate, I couldn't take any chances. Sticking something on him seemed better than sticking something in him. I picked him up again with a gloved hand. I wondered how the Disciples felt about science that used Bind-oh.

"It's okay, big guy," I told the frog. "It's okay."

The frog's legs drooped over the sides of my hands, like a rag doll's. He pulled his eyes in, in sort of a blink, and then they popped out again as Leroy put a dab of Bind-oh on his head and dropped the chip on the dot with my tweezers. I held the frog for the required thirty seconds so he wouldn't touch anything and get *that* stuck to his head as well.

I'd brought along a motion-detecting camera with the

intention of setting it up where the stream and ocean met. Instead, I set it up near the spring, not far from where we'd found the frog. That way, I could monitor him and see if he had any friends.

"If we can't figure out a name for the island, can we at least name the frog?" Delphinium asked.

"Rana," I said. It was part of the species name.

"Bob," Leroy said.

"How about Caesar?" said Davy.

"Bob."

"It's the last one of its kind," Davy said. "What's a good name for something that's the last one of its kind?"

And that's when it hit me. "Alpha."

"That's not the word for last," said Davy. He sort of mashed his mouth together, the way he does in school when he's waiting for the rest of the class to catch up with him.

"Exactly," I said. I didn't want him to be the last of his kind; I wanted him to be the first.

Leroy shrugged again. "Okay. But we're calling him Alph for short."

Alph seemed to like his name. He watched us with his round froggy eyes, and he didn't seem afraid. I set him back on the ground near the stream.

He took a hop, a short one, into the water, but he didn't sink all the way down like he was hiding, just like he was getting comfortable. He seemed to be saying, "So, yeah. This is where I hang out." I guess after you've lost most of your species to a hostile environment, a few kids with a tube of Bind-oh aren't going to freak you out.

I watched him a little longer, to make sure the chip stayed where it was supposed to, while everyone else explored.

Alph didn't move much, except to puff out his throat and holler, looking for company. The only company he found was me.

CHAPTER 11

We went home empty-handed. Even though we'd been mostly successful—I'd touched an actual frog—it didn't feel that way. Leroy talked me into leaving some of the equipment behind so we wouldn't have to lug it back the next time.

"It's not like anyone's going to steal it," he said. "There's nobody here but us."

It was true. Even the banks of the harbor, where we sometimes saw out-of-work anglers, were deserted.

We stowed the canoe in Leroy's hiding place and covered it with dead branches. Then we rode our bikes toward home. Davy turned off at Highbush, and Leroy, Delph, and I rode together until Elderberry, where Delph peeled off. "Later," she said.

That meant it was just me and Leroy when we ran into Derek Ripley.

At least I didn't have the aquarium on the back of my bike. There was nothing suspicious about me—nothing except that I was with a known lobster killer and I was wearing my grandfather's hip waders.

"Yo, Slime Boy," Derek said. "Waiting on a flood?"

"It never hurts to be prepared," I said. My back still itched. Seeing Derek made me itch more.

He nosed his bike closer. "Hey, Varney, what'd you kill today?"

"Mosquito." Leroy's expression didn't change.

Derek reached us and looked down at my boots, which were dotted with globs of dried mud and sand. "Haven't been anywhere you're not supposed to be, have you, Slime Boy?"

"I was exactly where I was supposed to be," I said.

"I told my dad I'd keep an eye on you."

"Because he can't do his own job?"

"He does his job very well." Derek looked smug. "People like your dad make it easy for him to reach his quota. In fact, one more green ticket and your dad might be going to j-a-i-l."

"You can spell," I said. "I was worried."

"Don't test me, Goldstein," he said "You guys have been up to something."

We didn't say anything.

"I'll bet you were in the harbor, looking for more lobsters, which is a violation of environmental code RE 17: No persons, either willingly or unwillingly, may enter the water for any reason without proper authorization from the EPF."

Leroy shook his head. "I guess we'd better give up, Ahab. He caught us."

"What the—"

"But we've moved beyond lobsters," Leroy continued. "We're on to bigger things."

Even though I didn't trust him, I couldn't believe Leroy would turn over so easily. He'd had practice getting in trouble.

"What are you chasing now? Goldfish?" Derek said.

"Bears," Leroy said solemnly. I almost laughed with relief.

"Yeah, right," Derek said. "You saw a *bear*. In the water."

"In the woods," Leroy said. "I'm not saying it was a bear. Ahab was helping me figure out if it was a bear."

"Yeah, right."

"You don't have to believe us," Leroy said. He didn't even blink.

"If you thought you saw a bear, why didn't you call the EPF?" Derek said, his eyes narrowing.

"I didn't want to call if it was a false alarm," Leroy said, putting his hand over his heart. "Isn't that a violation or something?"

"RE 29," Derek said.

"We were searching for evidence," Leroy said. "That's why he needed the boots."

I tried to think what sort of evidence would require boots. I got the answer a half a second before Derek did.

"You've been wading around in bear dung?" Derek said.

"I didn't say that," Leroy said. "I said we were looking for it."

"Actually, we refer to it as 'scat,'" I said helpfully.

"Who's 'we'?" Derek said. "Scientific Posers of America?"

"But we didn't find any," I added.

"I'm still telling my dad," Derek said.

"Good," Leroy said. "Then *you'll* be guilty of . . . whatever it was."

"Violation RE 29," I said. "I'd check it out before reporting."

"You're lying," Derek said.

"Leroy saw something," I said. True, right?

"You should check it out," Leroy said. "I'll bet Ahab would even loan you his boots."

"I don't want your crappy boots," Derek said. It would have been an apt description, if I'd actually stepped in bear scat.

Derek rode off, not in the direction of the woods.

I looked at Leroy. "Bear scat? Seriously?"

"It'll keep him away from the water."

It was turning out that Leroy could build more than a good canoe; he could build a pretty good lie, too.

I stowed my boots in the garden shed.

Fortunately, I'd saved my shower time, the last I was allowed before I turned it over to Juliette for a week. The cold water helped, but not much. I was still covered with red welts. I toweled off and coated myself with salve before I went back downstairs.

Juliette was out with Derek's brother again.

"She really likes him," my mother said, live from Fantasy World. She handed me a glass of Amp, water infused with essential vitamins. It had a faint sour taste, but I liked it. I took a sip so I wouldn't have to answer.

"Do anything productive today?" my father asked.

"I rode my bike."

"Did I ever tell you about the time the Mellor twins and I biked to Canada? Sorest my muscles have ever been."

My dad does not have what you'd think of as a biker's body. But when he talks about the old days, I can almost get an image of what he used to look like, with his brown hair spiked into what he called a "fauxhawk." (Apparently, that meant he was too afraid of my grandmother to shave the sides of his head.)

The twins were his neighbors, until they moved to Minnesota. The trip was the last thing they all did together before St. Paul.

"We went through two sets of tires," my dad said. "Not that it was such a far trip. Tires were thinner back then."

I'd heard this story a million times, so it was hard to concentrate. My mind went back to what Derek said, about the tickets.

"Peter's dad—" I interrupted.

"Come on, now," said my dad. "You'll give me indigestion."

But I started again. "I saw Derek Ripley this afternoon and he wouldn't shut up about your tickets. He said if you get one more, you're in trouble."

"I'm not in trouble if I get another ticket," my dad said. His laugh was contagious, and I started to smile, too. Then he said, "I'm in trouble if I don't pay the tickets I've already got."

I looked over at my mom, and I'd be willing to bet she was already making a plan to pay off those tickets herself.

"Ripley's not even a real cop," my dad said as my mom stood up and walked out of the room. "You know better than to say anything in front of her," he said when she was gone.

"Why don't you just pay them?" I could feel the anger burning in my throat like I'd swallowed a firecracker.

"If I pay them, I'm just donating money to the Angus Ripley Vacation Fund. It's a farce."

But it wasn't the lack of payment that was bothering me; it was getting all the tickets in the first place. "Why can't you just try to fix things?" I asked.

"What haven't I fixed around here? The dispose-all? The sink? I even fixed your sister's what's-it—that bracelet she got in Michigan."

"That's not what I meant," I said, which he already knew. "You keep talking about how different things were when you were a kid. Why don't you at least try to make it better?"

"Like what? Recycling a juice pouch? Look, Ahab. We have some growing pains. Things will straighten out. Give it time."

I couldn't believe my dad believed the old government line. Maybe he really did believe that someone was going to cover the world with some sort of regenerative pixie dust and fix things (the Disciples were our best chance, if you ask me). Or maybe he was putting up a front. Maybe he knew, even better than I did, how bad things really were.

"You could at least pretend to care," I said. "Put things in the right bin. Something."

"Kid," my dad said. I hated it when he called me "kid." It made me feel like we were in a movie. "My contribution to this mess isn't even the tip of the iceberg."

"Because they've all melted," I said.

"Ahab," said my dad.

"Dad?" I said.

"Shut it."

CHAPTER 12

Mr. Kletter was my favorite teacher at Blue Harbor Middle School. But that doesn't mean he was above taking us on pointless field trips. The good thing is that he admitted they were pointless.

"Settle down, class," he said after we'd all filed in. "Try to contain your bubbling excitement as we travel to New Arcadia." Like the other teachers, he wore a tight-fitting shirt, black with three-quarter sleeves, and long black pants that looked like they were suited for running in sleet. Unlike the other teachers, he wore a Hawaiian shirt draped over it. It was red, with enormous yellow flowers that didn't look like they were based on anything remotely scientific.

He turned off the lights and passed out a bunch of pairs of VR goggles, which looked at least twenty years old. "Put them on," he said. "You don't want to be left behind."

I put on the glasses and stared into the blackness.

"Behold," Mr. Kletter said in a flat monotone. "Rehabilitation Center Field Trip. Engage."

The screen blinked to life and took us to a lab in New Arcadia, where a woman was standing, waiting for us. She had a sharp nose and a smile that looked too big for her face. An image of our class appeared on a screen on the wall beside her. As she walked, it moved with her.

"Hello, Mr. Kletter," she said.

"Officer Drejko," he said. "Thank you for agreeing to show us around your facility."

"I'm so glad to have you," she said. She led us past some statues of animals—a steel squid, a wooden cow. I didn't see a frog. "Though I'm afraid I'm short on company this week." She gestured to the side, where we saw a bunch of cages and a row of aquariums. All of them were bigger than mine. And all of them seemed to be empty.

"As many of you know, President Franco has turned her focus back on the natural world around us. And that world needs a helping hand. When we find a fragile species, we bring it here to our EPF facility, providing the highest standard of care imaginable."

"It looks like Aqua Alcatraz," I whispered to Davy.

Officer Drejko cleared her throat. I wondered if she'd heard me. "Here, we employ some of the nation's best scientists, who provide our fragile species with a vitamin-filled diet to make them stronger and more capable of dealing with the natural world. When they're stronger, we release them."

I raised my hand.

"Young man?"

"Is that why the tanks are empty?" I said. "Because you've rehabilitated the animals and released them?"

"Is that why the tanks are empty?" she repeated. She sounded like the hologram lady back at the Rec Box™. "They're not all empty. Let me show you over here."

She walked to the corner, stopping at a tank with a large, silvery fish floating near the top, its body arched.

On the screen, I could see Davy raising his hand.

"Yes?" said Officer Drejko.

"Is it dead?" Davy asked.

"Of course not," she said. "You see how its mouth is moving? It is being . . . rehabilitated. Now here"—she moved to a different part of the room, where we saw a small, striped animal curled up in a small, wire cage that was filled with twigs—"we have the chipmunk. These creatures are little scamps. They love to run and play."

I squinted to try to see if the chipmunk was still breathing. Davy raised his hand again.

"Yes?"

"Is it dead?" Davy asked.

The officer glared. Then Derek raised his hand.

"Yes?" she snapped.

"My dad works for the EPF," he said.

"Oh," she said. Her body relaxed and this time, the smile seemed genuine.

There wasn't much to see in the Rehabilitation Center, though Officer Drejko led us around the room twice.

Because the field trip was virtual, we couldn't smell it, but I was betting it smelled a little like the harbor. Officer Drejko introduced us to one of the scientists, who sounded like he'd bought his degree at a convenience store.

I imagined Alph floating around in one of those tanks. He'd have been better off hopping around in a Rec Box™. And he was definitely better off with us. If we were going to save him, we'd need to keep him as far from the EPF as possible.

After Officer Drejko said goodbye, Mr. Kletter let us finish out the period with a virtual earthworm lab.

"Do not be alarmed," he said. "That long, brownish shape in front of you was not manufactured in the school cafeteria. On your desk, you will see a stylus. Please use the stylus to select your incision point."

My lab partner was Davy, who was grossed out, even though the worm wasn't real.

"Don't give me that face, Mr. Hudson," said Mr. Kletter. "This one is, in fact, dead. And in my day, it was suckling pigs."

"Mr. Kletter?" I asked as Davy plunged his tweezers into the projection and pulled back a flap of earthworm skin. I pulled back a flap on the other side of the incision, exposing organs that looked like they were made of chewed-up pieces of gum. "Why don't we do that anymore? With the pigs? Or with frogs? My dad dissected frogs."

"As did I. But the school system has decided—in error, I might add—that there is no need to study a creature's insides if you have no chance of encountering the creature's outsides. If it makes you feel any better, you'll do rats in high school."

"Virtually?" said Davy, making sure.

"Of course. Though I dare say the EPF wouldn't mind lending us a few live ones for educational purposes. That's one population that shows no sign of decreasing."

We turned back to our worm, identifying the hearts, the gizzard, and the crop.

"If Mr. Kletter studied frogs," Davy whispered, "he might know about them."

"Know what?" We'd researched a lot about them, from eating habits to skeletal structure.

"I don't know," he said. "Vocal nuances. Where the dentary bone is. You know: *stuff.*"

With Davy's assistance, I'd set up the Alph Cam so we could all check in on him whenever we wanted. We figured with the four of us watching, we'd see something else: another frog, another animal. But so far, the camera had only given us a few images of Alph hopping across the screen. Most of the time, even if he was out of view, the tracker showed a red dot moving in the vicinity of the spring.

"And . . . time," Mr. Kletter called as class ended. "Drop your stylus in the bin on the way out. That's one beauty of virtual dissection: no dishes to wash."

"We have some questions about frogs," I said when everyone but Davy had left the classroom.

"Dissection?"

"Actually, I'm really interested in their mating habits," I said.

"Why?"

It was a fair question. Why would two of your best students suddenly be interested in the mating habits of a species no one had seen in Blue Harbor for twenty years?

"Research," I said. I thought about last year's report. "I'm interested in the effects of climate change on their breeding habits."

"Mmhmm." Mr. Kletter looked skeptical, especially since he hadn't assigned us anything we'd need to research.

"We're trying to get ahead," Davy said.

Instead of going to his One, Mr. Kletter went to a cabinet. "It may surprise you to know that I am not intimately familiar with the mating habits of frogs, but this might help." He handed me a bound stack of paper, a book, with a cover that smelled old and moldy. The book was illustrated, in detail, in full color. Chapter 7 was about the life cycle of a frog. I'd seen some of the information on the One, but it was different having it here, all connected. Davy looked over my shoulder as we read that a frog's mating season typically lasted two or three months, beginning in May or June. The season for bullfrogs lasted longer (which boded well for Alph), but there were way more males than females (which didn't). At least, that's the way it had been when the book had been published, back in 2021.

"Do you know what a bullfrog sounds like when it's looking for a mate?" Mr. Kletter asked unexpectedly.

Maybe, I thought.

"No," I said.

He cleared his throat and made a sound similar enough to Alph's errrrr that it wouldn't have showed up as "cow, sick" on a One. He started coughing, but we clapped anyway.

"We had some in a pond near my house, when I was a kid," he said. "Sorry. I'm a little rusty. I haven't done that in a long time. They're invasive, you know, bullfrogs. Not that it matters at this point." He handed me the book. "You can borrow it if you'd like. If you discover anything new, I'll give you extra credit. Not that either of you needs it."

"Poor guy," Davy said when we were outside the classroom. "I wonder why the ladies are ignoring him?" He was talking about Alph, though I guess we could have said the same thing about Mr. Kletter.

"There aren't any," I said. We'd stayed in the classroom long enough that the halls, usually choked with people, only had one.

"Awwwww," said Derek Ripley. He was really good at being where we didn't want him to be. "Which one of your wittle fwiends is having pwoblems with the wadies? Let me guess: all of them." Derek looked at the book under my arm. "*The Mating Habits of Frogs and Other Amphibians.*

Is that where you get your make-out lessons?" He puckered his lips. Then he said: "Your sister didn't need a book."

"What's that supposed to mean?"

Derek just smirked.

"Shut up about my sister," I said.

"I'm just saying, my brother's a good teacher." He puckered his lips and made a smooching sound.

"Shut it, Derek," said Davy. I'd always suspected he had a crush on Juliette, though he'd never admitted it.

"Make me," Derek said.

I shoved the book into Davy's hands, which were curling into fists. I pulled back my own fist and socked Derek in the stomach. It wasn't premeditated or anything. My fist acted like it had a mind of its own. I'd never hit anyone before. It made my arm feel sort of noodly. My gut felt that way, too, when Derek punched me back.

"Did that hurt, Frog Boy?" he asked, instead of calling me by my usual name.

I fell against the wall. My vision even blurred for a second. When it cleared, Derek was walking away from us.

"I hope my brother dumps her tomorrow," Derek called back. "The less we have to do with your family, the better. Your father's a joke. You know that, right?"

Davy put down the book and we both started after him, but neither of us got in another lick because Mr. Kletter stepped out of the classroom.

"What is this about, gentlemen, if I dare use the term?"

"A disagreement," Davy said.

"I was just telling a joke," Derek said, walking backward, away from us. "Goldstein didn't like the punch line."

When Derek was gone, Mr. Kletter said, "I'd hate to think you were spending your valuable time focusing on the wrong things."

"Yes, sir," I said.

He winked. "There's plenty I could say about that kid if I wasn't afraid of the wrong people overhearing it." He looked near the ceiling, toward cameras we couldn't see but knew were there. "Stay out of trouble. And let me know if your research turns up anything interesting."

"We will."

"And, Mr. Goldstein . . ."

"Yes?"

"Let me know if I can help."

CHAPTER 13

But there wasn't anything Mr. Kletter could do unless he was secretly harboring a female bullfrog in his condominium. I thought about telling him about our island, but it wasn't mine to share. Besides, even if he was one of the good guys, Mr. Kletter was part of the generation(s) that helped cause this mess. I wasn't sure teaching us to dissect a worm could make up for that. There were underground groups, like the Disciples, working to repair the government's mistakes. Mr. Kletter probably even belonged to one of those groups, though I doubted he was a D^2. If he was, he wouldn't still be teaching at a middle school.

Still. *Don't trust anyone over thirty.* People had been saying that since the 1960s. My expression was: *Don't trust anyone who's eaten a real cheeseburger.* That meant people like my dad. And my science teacher. If we were going to fix anything, we'd need to do it ourselves.

Leroy, Delph, Davy, and I had gone to the island four more times and hadn't found anything else alive—at least, nothing that wasn't supposed to be. We'd seen some scat. It wasn't from a bear, though. More likely from a rabbit. The pellets were small, almost perfect little balls. They looked like the kibble Davy's mom fed their dog.

I spent some time looking at the plants, especially the ferns. We even discovered blueberry plants, which Maine used to be famous for, though there weren't any blueberries on them. And we found air—cold air—that seemed to come from underneath an exposed tangle of tree roots near the bottom of the hill. It was almost as if the inside of the island was air-conditioned. My research turned up a similar phenomenon known as an algific talus. Except there weren't supposed to be any of those in Maine, and the talus part—broken rocks that absorb cold air and freeze it—was missing.

Meanwhile, we'd been watching Alph, who still seemed lonely.

My sister, Juliette, was lonely, too. She came home with puffy eyes after a date with Peter, and when my mom asked how it had gone, she said, "Fine." Only, no one says "fine" if things are fine. You only say they're fine if they're not fine and you don't want to talk about it.

She wasn't talking about it. Not even to her friends. Usually, I'd hear her through the door of her bedroom. But for two days: silence. Then, when I went to the plaza, which sits between the middle school and the high school, I saw Peter Ripley with Elise, Juliette's best friend since sixth grade. He had his hand in the back pocket of her jeans.

When I came home, I gave Juliette a root beer sucking candy. I sucked on one, too. It's good to have something in your mouth when you have nothing to say.

It was Davy who figured out a way to solve Alph's loneliness problem and, in a roundabout way, Juliette's, too.

We were sitting on his back porch, which was glassed in, with his dog, Rudy, at his feet. He was on the Othernet, a hacker network that uses, as Davy puts it, "a winning combination of smoke, mirrors, and anonymity to allow for honest, heart-to-heart conversations." Honestly, he should be in charge of their ad campaign. I'd been on it before, a couple of times, but Davy practically lived there. And that's where he saw the frog.

"Ahab, check this out. I found us a frog." His voice was high again.

"A virtual frog doesn't do us any good," I said.

"Not virtual," said Davy. "It's for real."

He called up an image and sent it beaming into the air between us. I did not see a frog. I saw someone wearing a white mask that covered all of his face. He was holding his hands in front of his throat.

"I hate to break it to you, but that is not a frog," I said. "It's, like, a serial killer or something."

"It's not a serial killer. It's sign language," Davy said. "This guy has a frog. A real live frog."

I couldn't figure out what he was going on about. "Even if he does have a frog, how do you know it's a bullfrog?"

"See his left hand? Horns. Ergo, it's a bullfrog." Most of the smart kids I know have extensive vocabularies, but rarely use them, unless they're writing. Davy liked to throw in the occasional "ergo" for everyday conversations.

"That could mean anything," I said. "'Go, team.' 'Rock 'n' Roll.'"

"It means he has a bullfrog," Davy said. "I talked to him."

"You talked to him," I repeated. "About frogs? Just like that?"

"We were discreet, of course," he said. "We found a secure channel. And get this: His frog is female." Davy did a little dancing thing with his feet.

"How do you know that?"

"I told you, I talked to him." The dancing stopped. He was starting to lose patience, which, for Davy, is rare. Not as rare as a bullfrog, but rare.

"So where is this frog?" I asked Davy.

"Canada."

"Canada?" I said.

"It could be close, Ahab. Closer than if he lived in Texas or even New York."

"It's a big country," I said. "There's a big difference

between New Brunswick and the Yukon." The US and Canada had been friendly once, but that wasn't the case anymore. "We'd have to cross the border."

"Just talk to him. *Semper anticus*. Always forward."

When Davy brought out the Latin, I knew he was serious.

The next afternoon, Delphinium and Leroy came over and Davy plugged a small, square device into the side of his One.

"What are you doing?" Delph asked.

"Disguising us," he said. "In case of trolls. We're just trying to find a private spot where we can talk. It's like playing hopscotch. It makes our origin harder to trace." He punched in a few commands. "New Zealand is nice this time of year."

We were in. A beam of light projected from his One.

"We take the names of animals on the extinct or fragile list," Davy says. "I'm Snow Leopard. The guy with the frog is Naked Mole Rat."

"Why would anyone choose that?" I said.

Delph smiled. "It sounds like something you would choose, actually," she said.

"White Whale, maybe," I said. "I would not be Naked Mole Rat."

"I almost forgot," said Davy. He handed out three balaclavas, even though it was a hundred degrees outside. "Protection."

"I thought you said it was a safe channel," said Leroy.

"It is," Davy said. "He said he'd find us at 3:07."

The channel stayed blank.

3:08.

"Maybe he forgot," I said.

3:09.

At 3:11, a guy in a black mask flashed onto the screen.

"Snow Leopard?" he said. When Mole Rat spoke, his voice sounded like he was gargling with some weird combination of milk and metal.

"And friends," Davy said.

"Are they trustworthy?"

"Are you?" asked Leroy.

"They're part owners," Davy said. His voice sounded like he was gargling with the same mouthwash as Mole Rat. "I'd trust them with my life."

"Do you have him?" Mole Rat said.

"We have an image. Show him."

I held up my own One and projected a moving image of Alph in the spring. Mole Rat's eyes opened wider.

"I underestimated you," Mole Rat said.

"Your turn," Davy said.

Mole Rat's head disappeared and in its place was an image of a frog. It wasn't close enough to tell whether it was a female, but the breed was right. The frog was perched on a rock that looked like it had been polished and buffed. Like Alph, she was alone.

"What is your asking price?" Mole Rat said.

"We're not selling," I said. "Will you sell?" Owning two frogs, breeding them, continuing the species; the Disciples would have to take me then.

"You couldn't afford her," Mole Rat said.

"How much?" asked Delphinium. I don't think she really wanted to buy or sell a bullfrog; she was just curious.

"One hundred thousand dollars."

"Holy—" Leroy said.

"Told you," said Mole Rat.

I didn't like where this was headed, especially since my mom never remembered to give me an allowance. I washed test tubes on weekends sometimes, over at the university. And I'd get a little more money for my bar mitzvah, but that was months away. Combined, it wasn't enough to afford even a leg of Mole Rat's frog. It wasn't enough to own a toe.

"And you'd give us a hundred thousand dollars?" Leroy asked.

"No. I believe your threshold for parting with your frog to be much lower."

"You believe wrong," said Delphinium.

"Are you selling her to someone else?" I said. "If we don't buy her."

"My goal is not to sell," Mole Rat gargled.

"What is your goal?"

"Continuation. Propagation."

"Would you be open to an introduction?" I said. "You retain your ownership; we retain ours."

"If you journey here, then yes, I would consider it."

"Where is 'here,' exactly?" I asked.

He paused for a long moment. Then he said it: "Wodiska Falls."

"Why can't you come here?" I said.

"Where is 'here,' exactly?"

I looked at Davy to see if he thought it was okay to say it. "Maine," I said, without being specific.

"I offer the proper atmosphere," he said.

"We have atmosphere," Leroy said. Delph nodded.

"I cannot travel to you." Mole Rat said that part fast, like he was trying to get to another part of the conversation. "If you can travel, we should move ahead. Time is of the essence."

"Why?" Delphinium asked.

"Time is always of the essence."

I thought about Leroy's lobster. It hadn't taken more than an hour for it to die.

I looked up Wodiska Falls on my One. It wasn't in the Yukon, at least. I had to figure out a way to get to Canada.

And then I did.

"We can travel," I said.

"In what? The *Swan*?" said Davy.

"Excellent," said Mole Rat.

"Give us a few days to make the arrangements," I said.

"It has been a pleasure," Mole Rat said.

That's not the word I would have used. Maybe I would think of a better one on the way to Canada.

* * *

"So, Dad." We were eating dinner, my whole family, for a change, but nobody was trying to make conversation. "My friends and I decided we want to take a bike trip to Canada for spring break. Wouldn't that be cool?"

It had been my father's turn to cook and he choked on his to-fish. "What?" he said. "No."

"You went when you were just about my age," I said. "You and the Melon brothers."

"The Mellor brothers. They were twins."

"Right," I said. "It's just: You made it sound like you had the greatest time in the world and I was telling my friends how cool it would be for us to do something like that—for us to do what you did."

My father stopped coughing and looked pleased for a minute. "You want to follow in your old man's footsteps?"

"Some of them," I said.

"Your father was older," my mother said. "He was in high school."

"Not that much older," I said.

"Things were different then," my mother said, acknowledging the thing she didn't like to acknowledge—that the world had changed.

"I don't know, Ahab," my dad said.

"You said that all this"—I spread my arms out, to encompass the world—"was just a blip. You said that things were going to get back to normal. And if things really are going to be okay, fine, I can wait. I can ride my bike to Canada next year, or the year after that. But if it's not going to change, if this is as good as it's ever going to be, then this is my last chance. This is the last chance for me to do what you did."

My mom stood up and bumped her legs on the table as she grabbed the plate of to-fish and took it into the kitchen. Then she came back and stuck it on the table again. Juliette had looked up at me the whole time I was talking. Now that I'd finished, she was staring at her own plate again.

My dad frowned like he was thinking, so I pressed on.

"We can take a bike pike for most of the way. We'll camp in certified campgrounds." I held out my arms. "We'll spray. No bugs will come near us. And you can track us. The whole way."

My father considered this. If I could turn him, then he could turn my mother. She sat down again, humming to herself, a nervous hum.

"Who's going on this cross-country tour?" my father asked.

"Davy, Delphinium, and Leroy Varney." I didn't add "and Alph."

"You seriously expect me to let you go on an overnight trip with a girl?" my dad said. "Isn't Leroy the kid who got in trouble with the EPF?"

"*You're* in trouble with the EPF," I said.

"Wise guy."

"And Delphinium isn't a regular girl," I said. I wasn't sure how she'd feel about hearing that.

"I don't want you going out there unchaperoned," my mother said. "Without a responsible party. I'm not sure I want you going out there at all."

"We'd be safe."

"How do you know?" my mother said. "Nobody does this kind of thing anymore. Just the crazies."

"Dad did it," I said.

"More than thirty years ago."

"I'd do it again," my father said. "If I could." I thought about that, my dad on a bicycle with the rest of us, sharing a tent. Snoring. It wasn't ideal. But maybe—

"I couldn't get the time off," my father added. "You'll have to think of another chaperone."

"Wait. You mean you'll let me go on this trip if we can find a chaperone?"

"No," my mother said. "Absolutely not."

But my father shrugged. A shrug was only a gesture or two away from a nod, and a nod meant a yes.

But a chaperone? Who would my parents think was responsible enough to take four middle school kids to Canada and back?

Juliette reached across the table for the salt substitute and poured it over her to-fish. She put the shaker down so carefully, it didn't make a sound when it hit the table.

"I'll go," she said.

CHAPTER 14

If she weren't my sister, Juliette would have been the perfect choice. She could do no wrong in my parents' eyes. Her grades were above average, she called if she was coming home late, and she'd held a part-time job for the last two summers at a place named Nice to Soy You. Plus, she'd already been accepted into Welch College, where she planned to major in business in their low-residency program. That meant that she'd go away to school four times a year, for ten days at a time. The rest of the time, she'd attend classes virtually, which would save my dad buckets of money, thus elevating her to an even higher status. Grown-ups loved her.

But she was my sister. She didn't call me Slime Boy, but she'd called me a whole lot of other things that were almost as bad. When I fell in the harbor and had been possibly exposed to the Renegade Amoeba, she didn't give me her shower time without making me pay. I had no doubt she'd make me pay for this, too. But when she signed on to our trip, my dad officially came over to our side. We worked on my mom next. It was Juliette who got her to come around, after a whispered conversation. Leroy's parents signed on next, along with Delph's. Davy's mom was the only holdout. In a way, Davy was a holdout, too.

"Maybe I can just go virtually," he said. We were crouching by the spring while Delphinium and Leroy were exploring.

"It's not the same virtually," I told him.

"That's the point," Davy said. "Mistakes matter more in the flesh. Where you can see people. And they can see you."

"We're not making a mistake," I said. "We're introducing two frogs."

"You're not supposed to take wildlife to other states," he said. "Or other countries. We could cross-contaminate and wipe out the species."

"It's already wiped out," I said. "Anyway, you're the one who discovered the other frog." In our friendship, I had a lot of ideas. Davy made them happen.

"That was different," he said. "That was in the ether. Not in real life."

I thought about the games Davy played in the ether. Games where you could plan a whole world and fix it up however you wanted. This was a chance to do that, sort of.

"They brought pandas to the US all the way from China," I said.

"Foxes?"

"A type of bear," I said. I called up an image on my One

and a panda lumbered through the air between us, cocking its head to the side.

"They're gone?" Davy asked.

I nodded.

From the creek, Alph made the ERRR sound.

"Yeah, all right, then," Davy said. "If my mom says it's okay."

My dad talked to Mrs. Hudson for us. It was the last thing I expected.

"Listen, Kim," he said. He'd used his own One, which was better than mine, and proof that he didn't hate all technology. I could imagine his big, round face in the Hudson's living room, lifelike, instead of pixelated. "It's not like they're going to be completely on their own. Juliette's a responsible girl."

"I don't know, Ted. It's a scary world out there. People who spend time outside? They are not normal people."

"With today's technology, it'll be almost like you're riding along with him," my dad pointed out. "You can keep track of him, you can see him. Heck, you can practically kiss him good night."

There was more, but I'm pretty sure that was the line that convinced her.

"You'll have to check in with me three times a day," she told Davy. "At least three times. Am I clear?" We had to hand over our proposed route, which was close to the route my dad had taken when he and the Mellor twins had crossed the Canadian border, accommodating for miles of road that had been washed out. And we had to find covered, state-certified bike pikes with cool air. We had to swear to wear our helmets and protective clothing, that we wouldn't go too fast, that we would look both ways, and that we'd call the emergency number if we saw anything suspicious. Other than that, we were supposed to enjoy what Mrs. Hudson called "the freedom of youth."

I designed the map for our parents, which included the official checkpoint for where we'd cross into Canada. There was just one problem: We couldn't actually go through the checkpoint. Alph was contraband. What if he croaked, right when we were having our bags checked? What if government officials impounded him? And us?

Mole Rat had pointed us to a wooded area, about two miles from the official checkpoint in Easton.

It seemed sort of obvious. Wouldn't anyone trying to avoid the government checkpoint head for the woods? But the way Mole Rat figured it, the station was small, and there were woods all around. People who were doing the high-level illegal stuff would pass through at night, under the cover of darkness. We'd be doing *low-level* illegal stuff and would pass through during the day. If anyone saw us, we could just say we'd lost our way and hadn't even realized that we'd passed from Easton into Gareth.

I wasn't sure when to tell Juliette. If she knew, she might

resign as chaperone. Maybe I'd tell her on the second day of our trip, when it would be harder to turn back.

Juliette tried to take charge before we even left.

"You can bring one small pack each," she said. "Satchels for the bikes. You and Davy carry the tent stuff; the rest of us will bring food and water."

"It's my trip," I said. "I'm the organizer."

"So organize."

"Well," I said. "I guess what you just said makes sense."

It wasn't until we were packing up our breakfast bars that I remembered something I'd seen on the family calendar. "Isn't this your senior weekend?"

Juliette shrugged.

"How come you're not going with your class to Massachusetts?"

"Delphinium and I have dibs on the orange tent," Juliette said, as if she hadn't heard me. "You guys get the blue one."

"The blue one smells like Dad's feet," I said. "What have you got against Massachusetts?"

"I'd just rather go to Canada," she said. "Two changes of clothes per person."

"Then it's going to smell *worse* than Dad's feet."

Silence.

"You'd rather go to Canada with us than hang out with your friends," I said. "Seriously?"

Juliette sighed. "Better Canada with you losers than to

the corner with certain nameless seniors." They had names, though. Peter and Elise.

"Well," I said. "It's nice of you to give up your break for us. So, you know. Thanks."

She smiled a little. "Three changes of clothes."

Soon, the only thing left to pack was Alph. But we had to catch him first.

Davy's mother wanted to spend every minute with him before he left, and Delphinium had to watch her sisters, so the day before the trip, Leroy and I met at the canoe and rowed to the island ourselves. We maneuvered the boat pretty well, the two of us. Maybe you didn't have to totally like someone to be good teammates. Even without Delph's "stroke, stroke," we got to the island quicker than we had with extra rowers. Of course there was less weight in the boat, so maybe it all balanced out.

According to my One, Alph was spending the afternoon basking in the sun on his favorite rock. But when I checked the screen after we beached, the rock was empty.

"He must have moved," I said.

"Of course he moved." Leroy looked over my shoulder. "He probably got hot. If I spent all morning on a rock, I'd be hot."

I switched to the tracking screen. The light was still flashing in the same place. The same rock. But unless Alph's mutations included invisibility, he wasn't there.

We started moving toward the spring a whole lot faster. I inhaled through my nose so Leroy wouldn't see how out of breath I was, then wondered how I was going to clock more than eighty kilometers per day on the bike.

I waded into the water to Alph's rock. I didn't even think about the possibility of sea lice. The rock wasn't as empty as it had looked through the One. I picked up the tiny transmitter chip and walked back to the bank.

"Your Bind-oh didn't hold," I told Leroy. I almost called him a moron, only I was the moron, for listening to him. We'd used glue. This wasn't science; this was arts and crafts.

"Hey now," Leroy said. "If you'd cut through that cheekbone or whatever, you might have killed him. *Would* have."

"I don't know why I listened to you," I said.

"Because my idea was better," Leroy said, though not with the usual confidence.

"Your idea was better yesterday," I said. "Today it stinks."

"It worked," said Leroy. "If you'd come up here yesterday and tried to catch that stupid frog . . ."

"If you think he's stupid, you don't have to go to Canada," I said.

"You don't want me there anyway," he said. "Why'd you even ask me to go?"

"It's your island," I said. "It's your boat." I didn't tell him it had been Delphinium's idea to ask him along. I turned the transmitter over in my fingers, like it'd give me a clue to where Alph was hiding.

My eyes jumped from rock to rock to rock.

"Ahab."

"Quiet, I'm looking."

"*Ahab.*" Usually, the words came out of Leroy's mouth like they were in no hurry to get anywhere. But the way he said my name was rushed, urgent. I looked up and saw him pointing. I drew an imaginary line from the end of his finger. A few meters away, looking like a piece of dead wood, was the second alive thing we'd found at the spring. Only it wasn't another frog; it was a snake. And it looked poised to strike. Its tongue flicked in and out of its mouth. It knew I was there; it must've. But it wasn't looking at me. The snake was staring farther downstream, where a pair of eyes was raised just above the water, staring back. So there was some good news: We'd located Alph. The bad news: He was about to be somebody's dinner.

Slowly, painfully slowly, Leroy grabbed a real stick and stepped onto a rock, closer to me, closer to the snake.

"Don't kill it," I whispered.

"You think that's all I do? Kill things? I'm just moving it."

"It looks like a copperhead," I said, keeping my voice low. "It's poisonous."

"Yeah, I figured."

"Because of the head shape?" That's how I'd figured it out. Seeing a snake in the wild was pretty rare—though not as rare as seeing a bullfrog. Mr. Kletter had an ancient poster in his classroom, warning us to stay away from the snakes whose heads were all angles; the safer ones had heads that were round.

"No," Leroy whispered. "I just figured if a snake was going to keep us from catching one of the last frogs in the universe and illegally transporting him to Canada, that snake would pretty much have to be poisonous. It'd *have* to be. Get the container ready."

I backed away from the creek to where I'd hidden my net and Alph's home away from home. Then I moved upstream to fill the aquarium with creek water. I threw in a little algae and some rocks. I had some live roaches that I'd found, but those were at home, in the gardening shed. I set the aquarium on the ground and held up my net, moving back to where Leroy was standing with his stick. We made eye contact, and I nodded.

Leroy took another step and crossed to my side of the stream. I tried to remember how poisonous copperheads were. If we got bitten, it didn't seem like the sort of thing I could fix with black salve. If we got bitten, we'd need medical attention. And we wouldn't be going to Canada.

Slowly, Leroy took his stick and edged it toward the snake. The snake moved, fast. Leroy made a sort of shrieky sound as he whisked the stick under the snake's body. He flicked it, hard. The snake went flying upstream as I brought the net down over Alph. He tried to jump. The top of the net moved up with him, then down. I scooped him up and put him in the aquarium.

I looked over to where the snake landed. He was stunned, but only for a second. He raised his head and looked at us like we'd offended him.

"Think we should go after the snake, too?" Leroy asked.

I wanted that snake, poison fangs and all. But there was no time. Besides, it wasn't like we were going to bring him with us to Canada. Davy would freak if he knew he'd even been on the same island as a living, breathing snake; there was no way he'd share a tent with one. And who were we going to get to take care of a copperhead while we were gone? My parents? Derek Ripley?

"I don't think we can," I said.

"Yeah, well. That'd really be testing your matchmaking skills, finding him a girlfriend." He punched me in the arm, so the water in Alph's tank jiggled a little. Then he started laughing, this happy, maniacal laugh, the kind that said we'd just done something ridiculous and dangerous and possibly even death-defying, but we'd come out of it okay. I laughed with him. We laughed the whole way down the hill, and onto the beach, and into the boat. I hoped we'd still be laughing when we reached the border.

CHAPTER 15

My dad gave me the satchel he'd used on his own bike trip. I expected some sort of sentimental speech about his legacy and the Mellor brothers.

"Here," he said.

Juliette probably would have been his first choice to receive this valuable piece of family history, but my mom had gotten her a new satchel. My dad's satchel was dusty blue and wrinkled. But it was stronger than my school satchel, and I liked the idea of having something with me that had already made the journey successfully. When I inspected it, I found a slim book with a marbled cover tucked into one of the pockets. I opened it. *Canada Trip*, it said. My dad was not known for being descriptive. But on the inside pages, I saw directions, maps, even sketches of the landscape. His handwriting was small and hard to read, but I decided to keep it with me anyway; it had made this trip once, too. Had he forgotten about it? Or left it there on purpose?

The morning of our journey, I lined one side of the satchel with a towel. Then I sneaked back to the garden shed and loaded Alph inside, in a portable aquarium, equipped with the air pump but without much room for hopping. I'd packed the roaches into a gauze envelope, and I stuffed those in the satchel next to his tank. I put some provisions for us on the other side, including a container of water, to even out the weight.

I met the others out front.

Davy's mom was talking about a camping trip she'd taken with the Girl Scouts, to an amusement park in Pennsylvania, where they'd camped near the train tracks. Leroy's parents were saying a lot of embarrassing stuff about being glad that Leroy was making friends with some nice kids.

Then the parents took a photo of us together on our bikes. Leroy's bike was more beaten up than the rest of ours, but, as we'd learned on our trips to the shore and back, he'd tweaked it so it was faster and maneuvered better. Davy's bike was the newest and didn't have a scratch. He didn't ride as much as the rest of us. I wanted to bring out Alph and let him pose with us, but that would have derailed everything. I needed to remember to restage the photo once we were on the road, and once we'd told Juliette the real reason for our trip.

"Be good," said my mother.

"Be careful," said Davy's mom.

"Send me a photo if Valentino's is still there," my dad said. That was an ice-cream shop where he stopped with the Mellors thirty years ago.

"We will," I said.

"Take care of my girl, now, Juliette," Delphinium's mother said.

"Of course," Juliette said.

Alph made a noise. Not a full-throated call, like he was looking for a girlfriend; more like he wanted to join in on the conversation.

"Excuse me?" my father said.

"Oh, that was me, Mr. Goldstein," Leroy said. He started drumming on his stomach. "I have a problem with my digestion."

Leroy's mother shook her head.

"I hope you're taking something," my mother said. "An antacid. A gut pill?" She hugged Juliette and then me and then Juliette again. "You're fine?" she asked, searching Juliette's face.

Juliette kissed her on the cheek, which was a dodge I'd have to remember. My mother could interpret it however she wanted, which right now was: *Of course I'm fine. You don't have to worry.* We knew she'd still worry. My mom wasn't quite as bad as Davy's mom, but she was close. She'd seen enough of the world to know what was out there, even if she pretended not to.

My dad put his hand on my shoulder. "Don't do anything I wouldn't do," he said.

"Whatever." Except for making this trip, I didn't do anything the way my dad did it. I never had.

"Walk with me," he said. He waited until we were out of earshot. "You want me to change my mind about you going?"

"You can't change your mind now." I sounded more confident than I felt.

"I am your father," he said. "So yes. I can."

We looked directly at each other. Finally, he looked away. "Go on, then," he said.

Leroy was the one who started pedaling away from everyone, before his "stomach" could make another sound. The rest of us followed him down the walk and up the street. When I looked back, our parents were in the road, sweating and snapping photos, except my dad, who stood with his arms crossed.

"I thought we'd never leave," Delphinium said. She pedaled past me, creating a wind that pulled the hair back from her face. By the time we reached the Harbor Way Bike Pike, a smooth path with a metal roof that wound through the countryside, she was in the lead.

Part of me wanted to catch up with her, but I was carrying Alph, so I thought about her instead, and about naming things. The island was still nameless, but I thought I might call my bike the *Pequod*, after the boat in Moby Dick. I hadn't read the whole book yet—just the first three chapters and enough of the summary to recognize that I was developing an Ahab-like single-mindedness when it came to frogs.

The bike pike wasn't in good shape. The roof, which wasn't painted like the one at school, was held suspended by a pole every few feet. We could see the rust. And there were whole sections where the roof was missing, a victim of a storm, maybe. Every once in a while, there'd be a fan or an artificial rock blasting cool air at us, but there were no walls to hold it in. And every two hundred meters, we'd see a sign that said something like YOU'LL HAVE IT MADE IF YOU STAY IN THE SHADE and WANT MORE FUN? AVOID THE SUN. Of course we were already out of the sun when we saw the signs. They would have been more effective someplace else.

As soon as we really got moving, Davy needed to pee. It was against a new environmental ordinance—I forget which number—to do it on the side of the road, so we stopped at Silver Mart, a small convenience store on the way out of town. They didn't have a lot of merchandise—it was more convenient to have items delivered directly to you—so the store was mostly a collection of bicycle and car parts and reasonably priced bathroom access. While Davy ran inside, I unzipped my satchel so Alph could have more air. It seemed stuffy in there. What if the pump wasn't enough? I sat down and pulled out my pocketknife. *Sorry, Dad*, I thought as I pierced the leather satchel. I cut a hole in the side, like a window.

"What are you doing?" Leroy asked.

"Air," I said. "But I need something to block it, so no one can look in."

"Yeah, you do." He looked toward the store. "Now would be good." He stepped to the right and planted his feet between me and the Silver Mart. I moved my head to see what he was hiding. The doors of the small building had opened, and Derek walked out with his brother. Oh. He was hiding *me*.

The Ripleys walked toward us. Peter was carrying a volleyball, tapping it back and forth in his hands.

I slapped my hand over the hole I'd just made.

"Nice bag, Slime Boy," Derek said, going back to my original name, even though Frog Boy was definitely more accurate. "Glad someone in your family recycles."

My sister had been leaning against the building, but she stood up straight when the Ripleys approached, as if she had a metal rod inside her spine.

"Is that how you're getting to Massachusetts?" Peter pointed to her bike. I guess she hadn't told anyone she wasn't going on the senior trip. "You'll save me a dance, right?"

"Drop dead," Juliette said.

He put his hand to his heart. "Juliette, I'm hurt."

Davy came back outside, holding a bathroom key, which was attached to a long strip of metal. He waved it at us as he ran to the back of the building.

"You're not bringing these guys on the senior trip, are you?" Peter asked.

"I'm not going."

"How come?"

Juliette faked a yawn. "Not in the mood."

Davy went sprinting past us again, to return the key to the cashier.

"So you're babysitting instead?"

As someone who was also our age, Derek looked like he wasn't sure whether to smirk or look indignant.

"They're more mature than you are," Juliette said as Davy came back outside. That's when Alph decided to do his thing again.

ERRRRRRR.

"Digestive problems," Leroy said.

"Real mature, Lobster Killer," said Derek.

Leroy didn't respond. He just got on his bike and started pedaling. I got on mine and met him on the other side of the lot.

Peter and Derek didn't follow, even after Juliette called Peter a name that my mom wouldn't have thought was in her vocabulary.

"That felt good," she said. "Well, not good. But better."

We followed Harbor Way past apartments, past kudzu and witches' fingers, past fields of solar panels, which farmers liked planting better than food because it had a guaranteed yield.

Juliette was in the lead now, pedaling so fast it made me think anger might be the world's best untapped renewable resource. We took the pike north, taking a few breaks and walking up some of the hills. Around dinnertime, we decided to stop for the night in a town called Heaven.

It was a tiny town, with a small "designated forest area," and a certified campground that had water (limited and for a fee), bathrooms (limited and for a fee), and a scenic overlook (unlimited, for a fee, and with a few optimally placed billboards that changed every twenty seconds).

By then, we'd gone eighty-two kilometers, which was a lot, given our lack of training. We'd taken our time, partly because of Davy, who rarely exercised, partly because of Alph, and partly because of the heat, which blurred the bike path into a dream. It was hard to imagine that my dad had gone this far on the first leg of his own journey, but that's where his journal said he'd stopped.

There was no one at the campground's entrance to register us—not even a hologram. Instead, there was a rusty machine with a spot for our fingers and a keypad so we could punch in the number of our tent site. Just looking at it would probably give us tetanus. MONITORED BY MAINE PARK SERVICE, a sign said. DISPOSAL UNITS AT NORTH END OF CAMPGROUND. PLEASE KEEP OUR FOREST CLEAN. And then, above that, another small sign. WELCOME TO ANGEL'S REST CAMPGROUND. THE TREES HAVE EYES: YOU ARE UNDER VIDEO SURVEILLANCE. On top of that was yet another sign that said, simply, PLEASE DON'T FEED THE WILDLIFE. And scrawled under that in black, someone had written: *What wildlife?*

The campground was nearly deserted, except for a family of six, with their guitar, and a couple that looked just a little bit older than Juliette. When we started to set up our tent, they went back to the check-in station. Then they picked up their own tent and moved it across the campground, without even folding it up first.

We spread out the tarps, set up our tents, and got a few amalgamated logs from the dispensary. Davy put a tablecloth, which his mother had packed him, over a wobbly picnic table.

ERRRRRRRRRRR.

Leroy slapped his hand over his stomach.

ERRRRRRR, said Alph again.

"Are you going to do that all night?" Juliette asked Leroy.

Leroy shrugged. "Depends on what we eat for dinner."

"Hand over the water," Juliette said, moving toward my satchel.

"I already unloaded it."

"Then what's in there?"

I let out a breath. She was going to have to find out and we were a whole day away from home. "Leroy's indigestion," I said.

She looked at me like I was speaking Portuguese.

"I'll show you in the tent." If the campground was really under surveillance, I didn't want to take any chances.

Juliette rolled her eyes, but she followed Delph, Leroy, and Davy through the flap into the girls' tent. I lifted my satchel off the back of my bike and joined them. The sun hadn't set yet, and the walls of the tent seemed to glow a little. I lifted out Alph's aquarium and set it down in the middle.

Juliette leaned close to the ground so she could check out Alph from the side instead of through the screen on top. He moved toward her. "What is that?" Juliette said.

"A bullfrog," I said. "They're rare."

"I know it's a frog," she said. "I mean what—where did you even get it?" She looked straight at Leroy. I guess I might've looked at Leroy, too. He was new to our group, and the lobster story had been all over town. Plus, it was his stomach issues that had been covering for Alph's croaks.

"We found it," I said. "Him, actually. It's a boy."

"Congratulations."

"Yeah, well."

"I've never even—" She put her hand on her throat.

"His name is Alph," Delphinium said.

"And we're setting him up on a date," added Davy. I wasn't sure how I was going to explain the rest of it to my sister, so I was sort of glad Davy did.

"A date?"

"Yeah," said Davy. He's more a blurter than an explainer. "With a lady bullfrog."

"We're going to try to mate him," Leroy added.

Juliette reached for the portable aquarium, which looked even smaller with Alph inside it. She lifted it up and studied

Alph's amber eyes. He was pretty calm, given that he'd just spent the day in a stuffy satchel on the back of a bicycle. "Well," she said finally, "at least someone's got a social life. Where'd you find him?"

"Around," I said.

"Around where?"

"Around the harbor," I said.

"I didn't think they lived in salt water," she said, which was more than I thought she knew about frogs. Her eyes flickered, like she was calculating. "Would this be around the time you needed an emergency shower?"

"Around then, yes."

"And where's this hot date?"

"Wodiska Falls," I said.

"We're going to see Mole Rat," said Davy. "He owns the girlfriend. But it's a secret. You can't tell anyone."

"I can't tell anyone that we're going to see a mole rat who owns a frog?" she repeated. "Gee, I don't think that'll be a problem."

"It's a code name," Davy said.

Juliette was quiet, taking it all in. She looked in the direction that would have been home, and I wondered, for a minute, how much talking I was going to have to do to keep her from turning back.

"So the reason you wanted to take this trip," she said finally, "was because you're playing matchmaker to a pair of frogs?"

"It wasn't the only reason," I said. I thought about the Disciples and wondered if they took chaperones. "This really is our only chance to take a trip like this. And we really are following Dad's old route." Mostly.

Juliette nodded, once. "Make the fire," she said. "I'm starving."

"Whew," Davy said out loud. We'd gotten off easy. I hoped Juliette would be just as unflappable when I told her we had to sneak across the border. I figured that part could wait until we got there.

CHAPTER 16

Scientifically, the night sky in the middle of nowhere is pretty much the same as the night sky at home. What's different is the way you see it. What's different is how you feel.

Last fall, Davy and I went to the harbor with my telescope to look at the stars. There'd been no light pollution, and it had felt like we were in a different universe instead of three kilometers from home.

The universe above Heaven felt even more different than that one. The sky seemed clearer. The stars seemed sharper.

"There are so many," Delphinium said. She sounded breathless, like each star had taken a bit of air from her throat and made it hard for her to breathe. Except in a good way.

Juliette stared at the fire instead of the stars. Leroy covered the hole in my satchel with a piece of gauze from the first aid kit Davy's mom made us pack, and his famous tube of Bind-oh. Then he lay back on the bare ground, arms behind his head, looking up. "I'll bet we're setting the world's record for length of time outside," he said. "Hey. Shooting star! Did you see that?"

"You get a wish," Delph said. "Close your eyes."

I had about a thousand wishes I would have made. I hoped none of Leroy's wishes had to do with Delphinium.

"I missed it," said Davy.

"You'll get the next one," Delph said in that encouraging way she had. It was good to have her on your side because even if you weren't winning, she had a way of making you feel like you might.

"A shooting star isn't really a star, anyway," Davy said. "Just dust and other particles. But that doesn't sound as good. 'Shooting particles.'"

"It sounds like a band name," I said. They could play with Renegade Amoeba.

"I'll stick with stars," said Delph.

"Suit yourself," said Davy. Then, more excitedly, "I can't believe we're here. Alone in the forest." I guess some people would feel scared being alone in the woods at night. But to me, it felt safer. Especially with my friends.

"I'd better check in with my mom," said Davy.

"Bro, can't you hack her One or something?" asked Leroy. "Make her think she's talking to you when she's not? That's what they do in movies."

"Working on it," Davy said. He took his One out of his pocket and walked away from us.

"My parents were glad to get me out of the house," Leroy said.

"How come?" asked Delph. Of course.

"My brother's hard to handle. Well, we both are. I think they liked the idea of having just one of us to deal with, after the whole lobster thing. They didn't much like the EPF hanging out on their front porch. Also"—he added this last part like he thought twice about saying it—"my parents thought you might be a good influence."

I remembered what Mrs. Varney had said about being glad Leroy was with nice kids. "Why would they think these guys would be a good influence?" Juliette asked.

She was teasing, but Leroy answered seriously. "They see their names on the announcements from school all the time. 'Delphinium Perez pitches a no-hitter.' 'Jonathan Goldstein wins Science Fair.' 'David Hudson scores a hundred and seven percent on National Latin Exam.'"

"It wasn't a hundred and seven," Davy said as his mother's face dissolved into darkness. "It was a hundred."

"My dad thought some of that might rub off on me," Leroy said.

"You don't even take Latin," Davy said. Most kids didn't take a language, given that the One worked as a real-time translator. It could help you speak one hundred languages instead of just one. "You're in band and tech."

I wondered how Davy knew that. He probably did a background check.

"Maybe you'll rub off on *us*," Delph said. "Tell your parents that."

Rub off, I thought. It would make a good insult. I scanned the sky for another shooting star so I could make my own wish, which would be to unwish whatever wish Leroy Varney might have made about Delphinium.

Delphinium and Juliette crawled into their tent to get ready for bed.

It was quiet enough to hear the trees creak and the family with the guitar singing together, though not in harmony.

I opened my dad's journal. I was still surprised he'd left it for me and not for Juliette. Except. Except I think he knew this was my trip. I turned to a page with a doodle of a pine tree and the words: *Stopped in Heaven for night. (Not the real Heaven.) Hot but bearable. Raccoon stole our breakfast.*

There weren't a lot of details. I put some stats on the back of the page: how far we'd traveled, where the cooling stations had been out of order. It was weird to write instead of to dictate into my One. I wasn't big on details, either. I wanted enough data to share in a report to the Disciples, but not enough to serve as evidence if we got caught. I put the book back in the satchel and started to drift off to sleep to the pulsing sound of real crickets. And then: ERRRRRRR.

"Shhhh," I hissed.

"Digestive problems!" Leroy yelled out, in case anyone else in the campground was listening.

"Good night, Alph," Delphinium called from the girls' tent. In the stillness, it sounded like she was right next to us.

"Good night," Leroy said, in a sort of burpy voice, which did sound a little froglike. Alph answered him.

"That's not helping," I said, sitting up.

ERRRRR.

"Is he going to do that all night?" called Juliette. Whatever affection she'd generated for our frog was eroding.

Alph croaked again and again—way more than he'd croaked on the island. But then, we'd only been on the island during the day. Frogs were more active at night.

"He's lonely," said Delphinium.

"Not everybody is going to believe it's my stomach," Leroy said.

"Nope. They'll think it's your butt," Davy said.

"Wait." I had an idea. It was simple, but sometimes those were the ideas that worked the best, like (but unlike) Leroy's Bind-oh. The idea was this: If frogs were less active during the day, maybe all we needed was a little bit of light. Then Alph would think it *was* day and he'd talk less.

"That means we have to sleep with the light on," said Leroy.

"Why not?" Davy said. "You know. For the frog." Davy hadn't spent much time away from home. I think the sounds—of the crickets, of the trees rubbing up against one another—were getting to him. I remember the first time he spent the night at my house, when I was nine and he was eight. He was nervous about going to sleep, so both of us stayed awake all night. He fell asleep in the pancakes.

"For the frog," I agreed. Frogs didn't sleep much, from what I'd read. But I kind of liked the idea of Alph staying up all night, watching over us.

I set my flashlight near the tank. Above us, dark shapes settled on the fly of the tent. I watched the shadows move, trying to figure out the type of insect from its silhouette.

Wide awake again, I flipped through a few more pages of my dad's journal. When they crossed into Canada, I noticed a few French words, like *sud* and *nord* and *vélo*. On one page, he'd written a single word. *Stars!* Had he looked up at the sky, like me, with his mind completely blown? Even though we weren't in Canada yet, I wrote on the page next to it:

Yes.

He'd left some pages blank, but near the end of the book, I found whole paragraphs instead of words. I moved closer to the light shining on Alph's tank and read, in my dad's cramped handwriting, what might have been his teenage manifesto.

Saturday, July 21

189 countries are headed to Canada for the World Environmental Summit and the US isn't going. China's going. YEMEN is going. But we're not going because President

Tidwell says we can no longer sacrifice for the rest of the world. He says it's time for everyone else to catch up with us and even though blah blah we agree in principal blah blah science is inexact blah blah so we're staying home. Blah. It was a stupid speech. Therefore we, the undersigned, are appointing ourselves representatives for the US.

Teddy Goldstein
Chris Mellor
Timothy H. Mellor

Under that, he wrote a pledge, labeled the *Planet Protector Promise*. I'd never heard of the Planet Protectors. They sounded like an environmental version of the Boy Scouts. I wondered if the membership extended beyond my dad and his friends.

I promise to protect our planet
To preserve its resources
And to promote environmental stewardship
wherever I may roam.

This conflicted with everything I knew about my father. But it was his handwriting, which was small and hard to read, it felt more like I was translating ancient texts than reading a journal. It was my dad before he'd turned into an old guy with a million and one environmental infractions. He'd talked about his trip to Canada as a joyride. He'd never mentioned that there had been another reason for going. Then again, neither had I.

In our tent, Leroy made a snoring noise.

"Is that part of his digestion?" whispered Davy.

I could hear Delph and Juliette talking quietly in their own tent, but this time, I couldn't make out all of what they said. When the wind settled down, I caught: "*Something something* with them?"

"*Something something* just friends," Delph said. I liked the sound of her voice, even when I couldn't understand it.

"Well," Juliette said. "At least the frog's going to get lucky."

CHAPTER 17

The birds woke us before the sun did. Usually, what I'd heard about birds (other than seagulls and pigeons) was grim: A marsh bird flying north instead of south (and dying). A horned owl taking up residence in a Rec Box™ (and dying). But something was still living out here, because at five in the morning, the birds started calling to one another. They had a lot to say.

We gave up on sleep at seven and built a small fire, boiling water for hot chocolate and soy-real. Juliette handed out raisins, five each. They looked like larvae, but they added a lot of flavor. Leroy beamed the weather forecast onto the side of the tent so we could all see it more clearly.

It hadn't rained in weeks. But that, apparently, was about to change.

"If we stay on the pike, we should be able to keep going," he said.

The rain hit around noon, drumming the pavement with hard drops that looked silver from a distance. Juliette didn't complain, even though we didn't have as much cover on the pike as we thought. We stopped for a minute. I stepped out from under the awning, even though the purity of the raindrops was questionable. There wasn't a cutoff like there was in the shower.

"Ahab," Delphinium called.

But I just stood there and let the water hit me. Delphinium stamped down her kickstand and came out from under the awning, too. She stood beside me, dripping and laughing, the water gathering at the end of her nose. We were connected, to each other, to everything.

The others stayed covered, but by the end of the next kilometer, they were soaked, too. The spray from our bikes hit our legs. Steam rose from the puddles that Leroy splashed through at top speed. Delphinium followed, her eyes bright, and the connected feeling disappeared.

"Why is he here again?" I mumbled when I caught up to her.

It was supposed to be a rhetorical question, but Delph gripped the handlebars tighter. "It was his canoe. Also? He's our friend."

I had enough friends. "Business partner," I said.

My legs hurt from the day before, but I pounded out a rhythm, like we had on the water. Stroke, stroke, stroke. Push, push, push. By thirty kilometers, I didn't feel the pain anymore. I barely felt my legs, really. By the time we stopped for the night to set up camp, I was filled with a weird, exhausted kind of energy. My clothes hadn't dried. I imagined no one else's had, either.

Juliette signed us in and waved her finger in front of the camera at Armstead Campground, which was just outside a former wildlife refuge.

No one else was around. I didn't even stick a light in Alph's aquarium. If he croaked during the night (the talking kind of croak, not the dying kind), no one would hear it.

Leroy and I walked up to the bathroom. The inside was covered with graffiti: *Earth was here. Want to serve? CONserve.*

On the hand dryer, someone had crossed out the ON in PUSH BUTTON, so now it said PUSH BUTT.

"Never gets old," Leroy said, standing under the dryer to try to dry out his clothes. I did the same. The sound of the hot air prevented us from having to make much conversation.

For dinner, we made stew, using dehydrated vegetable flakes that tasted better in the wilderness than they did at home.

We were all on our second bowl when we heard a rustling sound. A deer walked into the clearing of the next campsite.

"Oh!" Juliette said.

The deer's fur was patchy, and her ribs were showing, but she still walked like she was performing in a ballet. Her eyes looked soft.

Delph grabbed a packet of soy-real and took some steps toward her, walking as gently as the deer.

"You're not supposed to feed the wildlife," Davy said, quoting the sign that had been posted at the check-in.

"Soy-real has eight essential vitamins and minerals," Delphinium said.

"It's starving," Juliette added.

Delph poured the soy-real on the ground, and then backed away. The deer bent her head to eat. "It's a stupid rule," Delph said.

"They don't want the animals to learn to trust humans." I thought about the EPF lab. Not trusting humans was a good lesson.

The deer finished licking up the food and looked at us for more. She took a step toward Delphinium.

Leroy jumped up, put his thumbs in his ears, and waved his fingers around. "Arrronnnnnnnngggaa," he yelled. He jumped, then pounded his stomach, turning it into a drum. The deer lifted her tail and fled.

"Why did you do that?"

"I'm teaching her not to trust humans," Leroy said. "Just keeping wildlife wild. Or whatever the sign said."

I wasn't sure what was scarier: Leroy's face when he was yelling "Arrronnnnnnnngggaa," or the fact that he was making sense.

It was too hot to crawl inside my sleeping bag, so I lay down on top of it, thumbing through my dad's journal. One of the Mellor brothers—Chris—had snored, too. My dad had drawn a picture of him on one of the pages. On another page, he'd sketched a flower, but I wasn't sure what kind. He hadn't labeled it. I looked for insights between lines like best ice cream ever and didn't bring enough snacks, before flipping back to the notes about the environmental summit.

Used Planet Protector badges to get in. Didn't work.

Arrete = stop.

Guard gave us free T-shirts and sent us home. Will try to sneak in for evening session. Tim saw door that looked enterable.

Weren't all doors enterable? Was that even a word? On the next page, my dad wrote a single word: failed.

After that, it was back to food and sweat.

So that was it. He'd failed and forgotten all about the Planet Protectors. He'd quit. Though I did find, on the bottom of another page, another single word: *beauty*.

They must have been on their way back by then. And okay, maybe he was talking about Mr. Valentino's ice cream instead of the great outdoors. But I chose to believe he was talking about the world around him—and the world around me—as I fell asleep to Leroy's snoring.

The sound that woke me in the morning wasn't Leroy, though, or Alph or the birds.

"Make it stop! Make it stop!"

It was Juliette.

I abandoned my sleeping bag, which was damp like everything we'd carried with us, and unzipped the flap.

My sister was standing in the middle of our campsite, waving her arms like she was trying to fly.

"I have warts," she said. "From your stupid frog."

"You didn't touch the frog," I said. "Besides, frogs don't cause warts; that's a myth." Until recently, frogs themselves had seemed like a myth.

Juliette's arms stopped moving and I saw big red welts in the gray light of morning. The welts were touching one another and at the center of each was a small droplet of blood, where she'd scratched. They looked like a ridge of small volcanoes.

"It itches so bad," she said. "SO BAD."

I knew that feeling. Delphinium crawled out of their tent, her hair looking like she'd brushed it with a tree branch, which was nicer than it sounded. "Maybe it's poison ivy?" She looked pleased to be able to study a rash in person. She took out her One and scanned my sister's arm. We waited, hoping it wasn't another thing that would make us have to turn around.

"Aedes albopictus," the One said. "Mosquito bites."

My sister's eyes got wide and she did that flare-y thing with her nostrils.

"It was probably just a GMO mosquito," I told her. The

government had been releasing genetically modified mosquitoes by the millions to try to get rid of the dangerous ones. They'd succeeded, too. For the most part.

"I've had mosquito bites," Juliette said. "They didn't look like *this*."

"Maybe you got too many at once? It could be an allergic reaction," Delph said.

"Exactly," I said.

"I thought you were supposed to be a frog scientist, not a doctor," Juliette said. Delph handed her some cream, and she slathered it on. "It's not doing anything."

"You didn't give it a chance."

"It's still not doing anything."

I reached down, got some dirt, and mixed it in my palm with water from my thermos. I smeared it on Juliette's arm.

"Jerk," she said. But it must have helped, because she dipped her own fingers into my palm and grabbed another glop.

"We should get you some allergy pills," Delph said. She grabbed the first aid kit and riffled through it. "There's only one here. We could have some delivered." Usually, there were nearly as many ADS (Automated Delivery Systems) as bugs in the sky, but not here.

"It'll cost us," I said. "Let's just stop in the next town. That's where Valentino's is anyway." I'd been humoring my dad when I said we'd visit. But he'd drawn a picture of the storefront in his notes. And we *were* in the neighborhood.

"I can't go into town like this," Juliette said. She scratched her arm again and left a streak of blood, which mixed like paint with the mud. But she helped Delphinium move the tent to the sun to try to dry it out before they packed it up. They found a hole in it, which must have been how the mosquitoes got in. Leroy patched it with gauze, like he'd used on my satchel. Great. Score another point for Leroy.

I tucked Alph into my bag while Davy talked to his mom again. I think that's one reason we bonded back in elementary school: Both of us had parents with high anxiety. We both wore raincoats when the forecast called for it. But while his mom showed her anxiety by calling every five minutes, mine showed it by pretending everything was okay.

When the conversation was over and our stuff was a little drier, we followed the path out of camp, riding along the empty streets. We found a store with medicine for Juliette. And we found Valentino's. The building was old and weathered-looking and the wood seemed to be held in place by thick coats of white paint. The sign out front wasn't lit, but you could tell it had been once. The red had faded to a light pink.

I took the satchel off my bike and we walked to the door, which was open, a little, even though the sign on it said CLOSED. I pushed the door open a little more.

"Hello?"

A bell on the handle jingled.

"It's like we're going back in time," said Delph. The barstools were orange, a sticky sort of plastic. The posters on the wall dated back to the early part of the century. And the guy behind the counter dated back further than that.

"It's early for ice cream," he said. "Don't you kids have someplace to be?"

"It's spring break," Leroy told him. He patted out a rhythm on his chest, a human beatbox. "Uh, you open?"

"Could be," said the man, who must have been Mr. Valentino. I got the feeling nobody had given him business in a while, given the empty streets.

"Our dad visited here a long time ago," said Juliette. She still had mud on her arms. "He said we should stop in if you were still . . . open." I got the feeling she meant to say "alive," because Mr. Valentino looked like he was definitely a fragile species.

"Did he, now?" he said. "I used to get a lot of kids in those days. Not so much lately. Well, if your dad said to come, we can't let him down, can we? I'm open."

The menu on the wall described ice cream and shakes and sodas. "I just keep that for sentimental reasons," the man said. "My real menu's here." He pointed to a small screen on the wall, where *ice cream* was now in quote marks. Delph ordered a blueberry cone, a Mainer thing to do, even if blueberries were hard to come by. Juliette ordered blueberry, too. Davy and Leroy went for chocolate. I ordered banana, because when you're dealing with fake flavors, fake banana is always the best. It was good to sit inside in the artificial air. I could picture my dad sitting on a stool, licking his own banana cone.

"My wife used to keep scrapbooks of the kids who stopped in on their way across the border," said Mr. Valentino as he handed out the cones. "Is that what your dad was doing?"

I nodded, and he handed me a computer tablet so ancient, I couldn't imagine the screen would even light up. My hands were already sticky from the ice cream. I wiped them on my T-shirt.

"You just click on that arrow and it'll take you through the pictures," he said. "Goes back forty years, that one. You can scan by the date, if you know it."

Juliette, whose hands were less sticky, started looking through the photos.

"Ahab, look!" I looked, and there was my dad's face, filling the screen with two boys who had to be the Mellor brothers. I couldn't figure out which thing was weirdest. The fact that my dad was:

(A) skinny,

(B) laughing, or

(C) wearing a T-shirt that said SAVE THE WORLD.

"Can we forward this?" Juliette asked.

"Afraid it's too old to be a part of the network," Mr. Valentino said. "But you can copy it." He looked at the screen. "They look familiar. Came by twice, as I recall. Full of themselves on the way up. Drowned themselves in milkshakes on the way home."

Juliette scanned the photo with her One and sent it on to my dad. When she finished her cone, she went in the bathroom and washed the mud off her arms. She coated them with pink lotion she'd gotten at the drugstore and came back to the counter.

From his satchel, Alph croaked. It sounded weaker than his croaks that first night of the trip. The jostling around was getting to him.

"Now, *that* is familiar, too," the man said.

"It's my digestion," Leroy said.

The man gave a bark-like laugh. "Is that what you call it?" he said. "Son, you can fool some of the people some of the time, but you cannot fool a Valentino. You kids heading to the border, too, ay? Wouldn't be bringing something you're not supposed to have?"

"Us?" Leroy said.

Mr. Valentino let out another laugh, and a whoop at the same time.

"Reminds me of the old days," he said. "That's what this place used to be. A weigh station for environmentalists. Yessir. Did I sell ice cream? The best around. But *information*. That's the real reason people came in here. I'll bet you want to know the best place to sneak across now, don't you? Oh, I wish Mildred was here. People used to run back and forth all the time, you know. But we haven't seen anyone in years, especially after the Unfriending with Canada. You're going to have to let me take your photo, too. For the scrapbook. Where you headed?"

"Toronto," said Davy. He wanted to cover our tracks, just in case.

Mr. Valentino seemed to know it. "You've got a lot more riding to do if that's the case." He sniffed, angry, I guess, that we didn't fully trust him.

"Wait," Juliette said. "What do you mean, *sneak across*?"

"I mean you have to tiptoe," Mr. Valentino said. "Duck and cover. You can't bring Prince Charming here through a checkpoint, now, can you? They'd just take him to one of those whaddyacallits."

"Rehabilitation centers," I mumbled.

"Right. Those people don't know a frog from a chimp."

"Sneak across?" Juliette said again.

I tried to look innocent.

"May I see him?" Mr. Valentino asked, nodding toward my bag.

I looked at Davy, who shrugged. If Mr. V was going to turn us in, he already had enough evidence. Besides, I needed to check on my frog. I put my satchel on the counter and opened it. Alph stared up at us.

"Would you look at that?" said Mr. Valentino. "Would you just look at that? Ooh, he's a biggie. Takes me back, this critter does."

Alph looked a little yellower than usual. I dropped a roach into the aquarium. It crawled on the rock, avoiding the water. Alph didn't even try to eat him.

Mr. Valentino didn't ask to hold Alph, which showed he knew something about frogs. He went back to his electronic scrapbook and started punching keys.

"Lookit," he said. "See these kids? They went up to Ontario on a horse. *A horse*. And these ones"—he nodded his head up and down—"went to go find some bird eggs and bring them back. Kept an incubator in our back room for a week."

"What hatched out?" asked Davy.

"Puffins," said Mr. Valentino. "Cute little things. They named one of them after me." His face clouded a little. "Didn't live, though."

"Mr. Valentino," I said. It seemed impossible, but I had to ask. "Was my dad transporting anything when he came through? Was he trying to save . . . something in particular?"

"I don't remember, son," he said, looking at my dad's photograph again. "Could be he was trying to save everything."

That didn't sound like my dad. He was more likely to try to save a hamburger than anything else.

Even though we didn't ask for it, Mr. Valentino had a plan to get us past the border. He drew us a map on the back of an old receipt. "The river's a natural border, see? But this is a skinny part. You can cross. Otherwise, you'll have to go all the way up here, and sneak across inland. Either way, this is the road to take." He handed me the receipt, which had *Valentino's* in fancy script across the top. "Something to remember me by," he said.

We let him take our picture before we left, though we kept Alph hidden. If Mr. Valentino turned us over to the EPF after we left, we didn't want any visual evidence. It wasn't as good a photo as the one our parents took, and Delph was the only one who was smiling. Juliette looked like she belonged on a wanted poster. She also looked like she wanted to kill me.

CHAPTER 18

"Are you kidding me, Ahab?" Juliette said when we got outside. "I'm supposed to go to *college* next year. How am I going to do that if I'm in jail in Saskatchewan?"

"We're not going to Saskatchewan," I said. "We're going to Wodiska Falls."

"We're going home," Juliette said.

"What? No."

"Well, I'm going. I'm done."

"You're our chaperone." It was humiliating. I bet none of Darwin's Disciples had to have chaperones. If you asked the One, it said, "Darwin's Disciples is a secret society of scientists dedicated to protecting, preserving, and improving the natural world." Every time there was a great advancement, the name was there. "Reported to be a member of Darwin's Disciples, she would neither confirm nor deny . . ." It didn't say, "Accompanied by their chaperone."

"Then I'm chaperoning you right back to Blue Harbor," Juliette said. "What kind of chaperone lets her charges illegally cross into Canada? With a frog?"

"A good one?" I didn't know whether to:

(A) call her bluff,

(B) beg her to stay, or

(C) beg more.

"Have a nice trip back," I told her.

She got on her bike and punched some coordinates into her One. "You'd better be right behind me," she said. She sounded like my dad, except my dad might have thrown a joke in there, too.

"Mom's going to be mad if you abandon us in the middle of nowhere," I called.

"Oh, I think she'll see things my way," Juliette called back.

"I think it's time for you to make a move," Davy said. "Do something."

"Don't worry. She'll stop at the next corner."

Juliette didn't stop.

"Ahab," Davy said. "She didn't stop."

"She just wants us to go after her," I said.

"Fine," Leroy said. "I'll go after her." And he took off.

Davy and Delph looked at me. "We've got to get her back," Davy said.

"You can't talk to her," I told him. "Nobody can talk to her."

"Well, I'm going to try," Delph said. And then she and Davy took off after my sister. I straddled my bike and waited another minute, watching heat rise from the pavement. But nobody came back.

Demikhov's dogs. It was the worst swear I could think of, a reference to a Russian scientist who worked on organ transplants, but who also tried to create a two-headed dog. Finally, I took off after them, too.

Even with Leroy yelling, it took us half an hour before Juliette slowed down enough that we could catch her. When she finally stopped, she glared with eyes like a hellhound, if hellhounds were 1.7 meters tall, with curly brown hair and lip gloss.

Leroy was talking to her when I pulled up, but they stopped talking when I got there. I put down my kickstand and faced my sister. "I'm sorry we didn't tell you our plan."

Nothing.

"We didn't think you'd come if you knew."

"You were right," she said.

"Don't leave the mission," Davy said. "Please?"

"You're my sister," I said.

"That's not my fault."

"It's for science," Davy said. "And saving the world and stuff. Like on your dad's shirt."

"'*Saving the world and stuff*'? Very convincing, Davy. Very scientific. How are we going to save the world by introducing two toads?"

"Bullfrogs," I corrected her.

"I'll tell you what's bull. This. I cannot believe you were going to risk our lives for a stupid frog. People get shot sneaking across the border. It's not like you're going to save the species, Ahab."

"They don't shoot people," I said. According to my research, the border patrol didn't even carry guns; they carried long-distance "nummers" that made your body feel like it had gone to sleep. "They just tase them. And maybe we *are* going to save the species. Somebody's got to. Why not us?"

"'*Just tase them.*' People die from being tased. They go to jail for less than this. You're delusional, that's all."

"I'm not delusional," I said. "Stay with us. Let's finish this. Because I'm not going back now. And you shouldn't either. What kind of chaperone leaves a bunch of kids alone in the middle of nowhere?"

"What kind of chaperone leads a bunch of kids across a border in front of armed guards? I can't win."

If Juliette kept going, we'd never make it to the border before our parents came to retrieve us. If they did, there'd be no frog spawn. No Disciples. Maybe we'd avoid jail, but I'd be grounded for five to ten years, easy. I wasn't sure I could win, either way.

"You have to help," I told her. "It's the only option." And then, because I like to be exact: "Well, it's the best option."

"What are my other choices?" she asked.

"Giving up." I meant more than just this trip.

The effects of Mr. Valentino's air-conditioning were gone. The sun bore into our skin. It was easy to be angry in this type of weather. It was easy to explode. I looked into Juliette's eyes, to see how far gone she was, but she closed them, squeezing the handlebars of the bike like she was trying to steady herself. She opened her eyes again and breathed. Then she turned her bike so it was facing north again.

"You owe me," she said.

"I owe you," I agreed. Until she turned the bike around, I hadn't realized how much I wanted her to stay.

She didn't say another word, she just started pedaling.

"I knew she was an outlaw at heart," said Leroy, with his wide smile.

We'd lost a lot of time, so we pedaled in silence and made it to about forty-three kilometers before we reached the literal crossroads: Mr. Valentino's Way or the Way of the Naked Mole Rat.

"Mole Rat," said Davy. "What does he get if he steers us wrong?"

"Mr. Valentino seems like he's been around, though," Leroy said. I think he liked him more because he didn't charge us for the "ice cream." "I vote for the old-timer."

"Me too," said Juliette. I could tell from her voice that I was going to be giving up showers and a lot of other stuff once we made it home. "At least he's somebody I've met in person. He knew our dad."

"He barely remembered him, though," said Davy. It stung more than I wanted it to. "And I don't think Mr. Valentino's been out much lately."

"I wish Mom had come through here," Juliette said. "I'd trust her opinion."

My mother didn't talk much about her journalism job before product photography, so it was hard to know where she'd been. Maybe she'd tried to save the puffins. Maybe she'd ridden a horse. She'd probably at least taken pictures of them.

"What if Mr. Valentino has a deal with the border patrol?" Delphinium said. "What if he's giving us a false map so that we'll get in trouble?"

The sun came through the trees and made me think of a poem we'd learned in English once:

During the day
Dappled sunlight
During the night
Splintered stars . . .

"We have to choose," Leroy said. "I say we go Mr. Valentino's way."

There'd been a note in my dad's journal, next to best ice cream ever. Gr8 guy, it said. My dad had trusted him. (Though there was also a note, a few pages later, that said TRUST NO ONE.)

If we didn't go Mr. Valentino's way, that left us following a path plotted out by a guy we'd never met who illegally owned a frog. A guy who illegally owned a frog *just like me*. And that was my answer. I had more in common with Mole Rat than with anyone—including my dad.

"Mole Rat," I said.

"Could have predicted that," Leroy said. "Let's put it to a vote. Who's with me on Mr. Valentino?" Only Juliette raised her hand.

"Mole Rat wins," I said.

"I'm the chaperone," Juliette said. "My vote counts more."

"Well," Leroy said, "at least this way we've got someone to blame if we get busted."

"That doesn't make me feel better," Juliette said.

"We're not going to get busted," I said. "We're going to go to Canada."

We started pedaling in the direction of the woods near Easton like Mole Rat had instructed us. We rode under the cover of trees, sweat still pouring off us. It made Juliette's arms itch even worse. I wondered why, if they could develop cures for Ebola and diabetes, no one could find a way to get rid of mosquito bites. We stopped in Geddy to get our bearings.

"We have to stay hushed from now on," Davy whispered. "Mole Rat said not to make noise."

There were patrol stations set up on each side of the river, and sensors that ran parallel to it. According to Mole Rat, most of the sensors didn't work; they were just there as a deterrent. There was a spot twenty-eight kilometers from the border station that was especially faulty.

I rearranged Alph in my satchel, turned on a cold pack to keep him cool and a flashlight to act as the sun. "Stay quiet, Alph," I said. I sealed him up.

My One showed when we were getting near the invisible line, though the rush of the water told us that, too. Leaves crunched under our bike tires.

Just stay quiet, Alph, I thought. *Stay quiet*.

You could hear the rattle of our bikes as we rode single file through the woods.

My heart beat faster. So far, so good.

And then, the silence was ripped apart.

"JUST WHAT DO YOU THINK YOU'RE DOING, YOUNG MAN?"

The voice was shrill, like a siren, but it wasn't the border patrol. It was Davy's mom, her life-size head glaring at us from between Davy's handlebars.

Davy slammed on his brakes. I was impressed he didn't wreck. I would have.

He made his own voice super soft, and we hoped Mrs. Hudson would mimic him. "I'm just riding, Mom."

This was the part of the trip I'd worried the most about—not just because we were sneaking across the border but because whether we followed Mr. Valentino's route or Mole Rat's route, we were veering from the route we'd told our parents we were taking. Mrs. Hudson was tracking us.

"I thought you kids had some sense, and that includes sense of direction." Mrs. Hudson didn't take the hint, about lowering her voice.

Juliette pulled down her kickstand and stood behind Davy, so Mrs. H could see her face. "There was a problem with the path—" she began, but Mrs. Hudson kept shouting. She was still shouting when two patrol officers approached us on scooters not so different from the one Derek Ripley's dad drove. They had helmets, the kind someone would wear on a safari.

"Piltdown Chickens," I muttered. That was the name of the fossil of a chicken that had been merged with the fossil of a dinosaur tail. It was supposed to be the missing link, before people found out it was a hoax.

"Are those officers?"

"Yes, ma'am," Davy said.

"You see what a wrong turn can do? It can get you arrested. You stand up straight and listen to them."

One of the officers—her name tag said Officer Kennedy—addressed Mrs. Hudson directly. "Border patrol, ma'am. We'll get them moving in the right direction."

"I appreciate you doing so," Mrs. Hudson said.

"I'll call you later, Mom," Davy said. "After we see what transpires here." "Transpires" was up there with "ergo" in Davy World.

"Five minutes," she said. "You will call me in five minutes."

There was silence.

"We couldn't help overhearing," said the other officer, Officer Liu. "Are you lost?"

"We were following the river," Leroy said. He was good under pressure. "I guess we got confused."

"Why didn't you stay on the pike?" asked Officer Liu, somehow overlooking the fact that getting confused by a river that only flowed in one direction did not say much about our level of intelligence.

"We wanted the road less traveled," Leroy said.

"What's your destination?" asked Officer Kennedy.

Don't say Canada. Don't say Canada. Don't say Canada.

"My grandmother's house," said Leroy. "In New Glaser."

That was on our side of the border. It was close enough that our "wrong turn" didn't look suspicious. Plus, New Glaser happened to take us near the road that Mr. Valentino had suggested. It was like Leroy had a grid laid out in his head instead of on his One.

Davy's mom had been a good alibi, too.

"ID?" Officer Kennedy said.

But not good enough.

Juliette held up her finger. "I'm responsible," she said. "If anyone's in trouble, it should be me." *But later, it's going to be me*, I thought.

Officer Liu scanned Juliette's finger, while she gave me the You're-dead-Ahab look I knew so well.

"Ah," said Officer Liu. "Here's your record." I wondered if it was full of gold stars. We were quiet as he read. Finally, he said, "Do you realize you're within half a mile of the Canadian border, Miss Goldstein?"

"Border?" said Delphinium, which might have been pushing it.

"Canada," Officer Liu said patiently.

"My grandmother lives near the border," Leroy said.

"Right," said Officer Liu. "But New Glaser is in *that* direction. You follow this path to the main road, and you'll be back on track. Aren't you following a map?"

I hoped he wouldn't ask to see the route we'd planned out.

"We're practicing using nature," Leroy said. "The direction of the sun."

"We're following the signs, sir," said Davy, his voice quiet, his back so straight I wondered how he could breathe.

There was a beeping sound, and the officer looked at his One and then at his partner.

"Murray, again?" she said.

He nodded.

Officer Kennedy looked at us. "That way," she said, pointing. "Got it?"

"Copes," Leroy said.

"Copes?"

"Copasetic," he said.

She nodded. Then she looked at Davy. "Call your mother. We have a lot of experience with mothers. Something tells me this is one mother you don't want to mess with."

"I'll call," Davy said. But he waited until the officers started their bikes before asking the One to engage.

"I'm not in jail," he told his mom.

"Thank goodness those officers came along when they did."

"Yes," said Davy. "They were very helpful."

I decided to let them be even more helpful.

"Don't forget to tell her we're changing our route slightly," I said. "So she won't worry."

"What?" Davy said.

"What did he say?" said Mrs. Hudson.

"The officers suggested a better route," I said. Now maybe she wouldn't scream at us when she saw we were off course. "A shortcut," I added.

Before we took off again, I made Davy change the setting on his One so we wouldn't get any more surprises from Mrs. H. I was sure Juliette would threaten to leave again, but she didn't. We kept on through the woods until we reached the main road. We pedaled past a small, abandoned wind farm, the turbines lying on the ground like giant metal moths.

"Are they following us?" whispered Juliette. She meant the officers, not the turbines.

"We count to one hundred," I said. "Act like you're scratching your mosquito bites or something. If we don't see anyone by one hundred, we cross the road and take Mr. Valentino's route."

Davy did the counting.

Juliette scratched her mosquito bites, probably pretending she was scratching my eyes out. I sneaked another peek at Alph to make sure he was okay. He wasn't moving around as much as he'd been, but the roach was gone. I wasn't sure if it had crawled into the sand pile, or if Alph had eaten it. Either way, the sooner we got to Mole Rat's compound, the better.

"Ninety-nine. One hundred."

There was still no sign of the officers, no movement but leaves and grass pushed by the warm wind.

"Okay," said Leroy. "Let's go."

We crossed the highway and moved onto the access road.

"Let's hope Mr. Valentino wasn't lying to us, like your friend Mole Rat," Leroy said.

"He didn't lie," said Davy.

"He got us busted."

"He didn't know they'd be patrolling."

"He should have."

All I was thinking about is what would have happened if Davy's mom hadn't yelled. We might have been caught going over the border—if not on our side, on theirs. We might, still.

"Mr. Valentino said to look for a ghost birch," Juliette said. "What the heck is a ghost birch?"

"A tree," I said. "With white bark." Blight had killed most of them, so there weren't many left.

"There!" Delph pointed.

A white tree stood just off the path. Its bark was peeling like it had a skin disease, and it looked like it had been struck by lightning more than once. Even in what was left of the daylight, it looked ghostly; I imagined it was worse at night. What I couldn't imagine was how Mr. Valentino knew it was still there. But we pedaled up to it and turned right.

"One hundred meters," I said.

"I cannot believe I'm doing this," Juliette whispered.

"Fifty."

The terrain didn't change much. There wasn't a wall, like there was on other borders, just a spot where the river was practically dry. I glanced at my One again, and we crossed the invisible line. No buzz. No sirens. No border patrol.

"Welcome to Canada," I whispered.

Did the trees look taller? I felt like we should stop and mark the moment, but that would have looked suspicious. Besides, we'd lost time by going the wrong way. In just thirty-two kilometers, if we kept at it, we'd be at Mole Rat's compound.

I hoped he hadn't sent us the wrong way on purpose. I hoped he had a girlfriend for Alph.

CHAPTER 19

I'm not sure what I expected Naked Mole Rat's compound to look like; I only knew when we pulled up in front that it was the furthest thing from what I expected.

For one, it was a house, a huge one. Three of my houses would have fit in one of his.

Mole Rat had a yard, too, but it wasn't filled with fake grass, like the yards back in Maine; this grass was real, tall, and out of control. In the light of the streetlamp, I could see thistles and pokeweed. A walkway went from the street to the front door, dividing the grass like it was the Red Sea.

"Do you think it's too late to ring the bell?" Juliette asked.

We'd set up at another nearly deserted campground and made our way over in the dark.

"He's expecting us," I said. I wondered if Mole Rat traded stocks for a living. I wondered how he got his yard to grow like that.

"He *was* expecting us," said Davy. "Maybe he isn't anymore." The house was dark. When we moved closer, the security light flashed on. If anyone was home, they knew we were outside.

I picked up the satchel off the back of my bike.

"Wait, you're just gonna carry him straight to the front door?" Leroy said. "What if it's a trap?"

"We could play a little hard to get," Delph said, agreeing with Leroy yet again. "Right?"

I set the satchel back on the bike again. "You ring the bell," I said. "I'll wait here."

"Fac fortia et patere," Davy said. "'Do brave deeds and endure.' He's been talking to me. I'll go first."

He went up the front walk, slowly.

"Oh, this is ridiculous," said Juliette. She pushed down her kickstand again and caught up with Davy. Delphinium followed on Davy's other side.

They reached the porch together, but it was Juliette who rang the bell.

The door opened and a woman my mother's age stepped out.

"Mole Rat?" said Davy.

"Pardon?" The woman looked at him like an alien had landed on her stoop.

"We're looking for Mole Rat," Davy said again.

"Oh," she said. "Right. *Mole Rat.*" She looked over her shoulder and into the house. "Simon?" she shouted. "It's for you."

For a minute, it was just the woman in the doorframe. And then someone else joined her at the door. The light behind him, from the front hall, made it look like he was glowing. But he was shorter than I expected, and when he spoke, his voice was a lot higher.

"Snow Leopard?" he asked Davy.

Davy gave him a hand signal, three fingers down, with the thumb and pinky extended up.

Mole Rat gave one in return.

"These are the friends I was telling you about," Mole Rat told the woman. "They're late."

On the Othernet, with the mask and voice changer, it had been hard to guess Mole Rat's age or gender. In my mind, he was a man, about thirty years old. Also, he had a goatee. This Mole Rat was only about 1.5 meters tall, with puffy cheeks. As I got closer, I realized he was a kid, probably near our age. The woman must have been his mother. She looked at Delphinium, who gave her a half wave, and at Juliette, whose arms were still covered with pink stuff.

It was a good thing, because Juliette could look like a fashion model if she wanted to, and Mole Rat's mother didn't look like the kind of mother who wanted her kid hanging out with a fashion model after ten p.m. on a weeknight. But without makeup and with the pink stuff, Juliette looked like a regular kid.

"Pleased to meet you," Juliette said.

Mrs. Mole Rat returned the greeting, then squinted into the darkness. "Are there more of you?"

Leroy and I stepped forward with the satchel. We stood there, awkwardly, a feeling I was used to. Finally, Mole Rat whispered something to his mother.

"Do you know what time it is, Simon?" she said.

"Mole Rat," he corrected.

"Do you have any idea what time it is, Mole Rat?"

"We're sorry about the time," Juliette said. "It took us much longer to get here than we thought it would." She pointed to our bikes on the walkway.

"We've been on the road forever," Delphinium added. "We took a wrong turn near Geddy."

"A very wrong turn," Leroy added darkly.

Mrs. Mole Rat didn't say anything, so her son leaned in again and whispered something else.

"You need your rest, Simon," she told him.

He whispered again.

"Oh. Fine, then," she said, and walked out of view.

"Come on in," Mole Rat/Simon told us.

He backed away from the door, stiff-legged, and turned. Then, with the same stiff-legged walk, he led us through the long front hallway and into a living room. It wasn't the sort of room that had a couch in it; it was the sort of room where everything seemed to be truly alive. There was furniture made of old vines and tree branches, and the floor below us was real grass. I looked up. While the outside of the house had made it look like there was a second floor, inside, there was just space—space that had been filled with trees and vines. The ceiling was glass, like an old-fashioned greenhouse. It was what the Rec Boxes™ dreamed of being. But the plants in the Rec Boxes™ were haphazard, with cactuses growing next to plants you would have found in the tropics, and plastic flowers to fill in the gaps. Here, everything belonged together. Here, everything was real.

"It smells heavenly," said Delph. It did—flowery and misty and warm. Delph reached out and touched an orange flower that looked like a gaping mouth. A small green pod that dangled near it curled inside itself and sent seeds spraying into the air. Delphinium caught the seeds in one hand and offered them back to our host. "I'm sorry," she said. "I didn't mean to break it."

"That's jewelweed," Mole Rat/Simon said. "Don't worry; it's supposed to do that. Here." He grabbed another pod and placed it gently in her hand. It split and curled.

A buzzing sound filled the room.

"Are those *bees*?" I asked.

Mole Rat laughed. "They're fans—mechanical pollination." He pulled a Q-tip out of his pocket. "I use these, too, sometimes."

Now that I looked more closely, I could see small fans among the foliage, their propellers aiming upward and sending a cool stream of air across the room. I turned and looked past the trees to a small, clear waterfall that emptied into a pond, with ferns along the banks. Apparently, it was the only waterfall left in Wodiska Falls. Only nobody knew about it.

"How is this even possible?" I asked.

We'd been to museums, government labs, and of course the Rec Boxes™. But nothing came close to what was going on in Mole Rat's living room. Even our island, which had its own magic, wasn't as lush.

"I have a green thumb," Simon said. "I'm also extremely resourceful and—" He took a breath. "Tenacious." He led us over to a table and chairs, sat down, and motioned us to do the same.

"As you might have surmised, I'm Mole Rat."

"Snow Leopard," Davy said again. "Also known as David B. Hudson. Well. Davy."

"Mama's boy," Leroy suggested under his breath, as Davy's One pulsed with light. I was glad he'd changed the setting so Mrs. Hudson's head didn't pop up in the middle of Mole Rat's living room.

"Excuse me," Davy said. "I have to get this." He headed to the generic background of the entrance hall, but we could hear Mrs. Hudson's voice coming out of his pocket until he got there.

"Geez, Mom, I've only been here for five minutes."

"Eight," said his mother.

"Leroy," Leroy said to Mole Rat loudly, trying to drown Davy out. "You can call me Squid."

"Delphinium," said Delphinium. No last name. No animal name.

"Juliette Goldstein," said Juliette. "And my brother, Ahab."

"Simon? Excuse me. *Mole Rat*," said Mole Rat's mom, coming back with a tray. It turned out to contain cookies. They came in reds and oranges and greens, matching the colors in the room. "I thought your friends might be hungry."

"Thanks," Mole Rat said as she set the tray in front of us. He sighed. "Okay. You guys may as well call me Simon."

His mom smiled at us for the first time. "I'm Mama Bear," she said. "But you can call me Mrs. Laffitte. I'll be in the other room if you need me."

Simon nodded again and she left.

"Ahab, look!" Delphinium was pointing to some bushes where two birds were perched. They were small and brown, not colorful at all. But they weren't animatronic, either, like the birds in the Rec Boxes™. Delphinium was caught up in the dance of their movements—real birds inside a house. But I saw something else: a warning.

"How can you responsibly own an amphibian with those monsters on the loose?" I said.

"Monsters?" Delphinium said. "They're cute. Besides, Alph could take them."

Simon looked at me smugly. "Are you referring to my vegetarian finches?" he said.

"Whoa," I said.

"Excuse me," said Leroy. "But for those of us who aren't ornithologists, what is the big flipping deal about vegetarian finches?"

Simon was silent. I guess he was waiting to see how much I knew. So I answered, "They were some of Darwin's finches," I said. I wasn't talking about the Disciples. I was talking about the original.

"Darwin?" Leroy said. "Theory-of-Evolution Darwin?"

"How many Darwins do you know?" Simon asked.

"They were found on the Galapagos Islands," I said. "Other places, too, and then, no place. They haven't been seen in—well, they haven't been seen, that's all. And they're true vegetarians. They won't eat frogs. They won't even eat bugs."

"I'd be more worried about the frogs eating the birds," Leroy said.

"I keep water for them away from the pond," Simon said. "They know better."

"Well," Delphinium said. "I guess that'll do in a finch." Things always felt less stressful when she managed to pull off a pun. "Owl be right over here," she said, going to where Juliette stood watching the waterfall pour over the rocks.

Droplets of water splashed on my sister's arms and legs. She looked back at me. It was a Where-did-you-find-this-guy? look. But I hadn't found him. Davy had. And now that we were here, my choices were down to two:

(A) Trust him, or

(B) don't.

CHAPTER 20

"Do you have any *more* questions about the safety of my ecosystem?" Simon asked. I'd moved on from the finches to asking about his use of fertilizer (compost) and whether he used chemicals for bug control ("duh, no").

"Give me a second," Leroy said. "I always have questions."

Simon bent forward to grab a cookie. Then he sat straight up again. His legs didn't move with the rest of him. I looked for a minute at his shoes, which were black and stiff—not sneakers like the rest of us were wearing.

"Why haven't you done something like this to our living room?" Juliette asked me.

"Like Dad would let me," I said. I didn't say: *Like we could afford it.* Because no matter how resourceful Simon was, an operation like this took money. Still, I imagined our couch, with its puffy turquoise pillows, replaced by a silvery waterfall.

"It would cheer up Mom, I'll bet," she said.

Davy, who had put his One away, was back and reaching toward the water.

"Don't touch it," Simon said.

"I thought you said it was safe," said Leroy.

"It is," Simon said. "But he's not. I don't know where his hands have been."

I grabbed a cookie with my own not-so-clean hands. It was sweet but rubbery.

I was aware of Alph, near my feet in the satchel. I wasn't sure about pulling him out. I could lose track of him in a big room like this.

"So now what?" said Leroy, helping himself to another cookie.

Juliette looked at Simon. "Where's your frog?"

"Where's yours?" Simon said.

I patted the satchel.

Simon pointed toward the pond. "There's a spot Elvira likes just behind the waterfall. Why don't you see if she's there?"

The frog was there all right. Simon's frog was a little smaller than Alph, with a slightly greener face but the same buggy, yellow eyes.

"So how do we introduce them?" Davy said. "Soft music? A movie?"

We looked over at Simon, waiting for some guidance. He rose and walked over to us.

"Perhaps you can introduce him to me first."

I brought over the satchel and lifted the top. Alph stared up at us through the lid of his aquarium. Simon smiled.

"Not that I didn't believe you," he said, "but look at the size of him!"

"Let's let him out," Leroy said. He looked at Simon. "Or will that mess with your ecosystem?"

I thought about that. The two frogs had grown up in completely different environments. What if they made each other sick? I was pretty sure Alph's sluggishness had to do with transporting him in a stuffy bag for three days, but what if it was something else? Our chances of renewing the species would be over. I thought about Mr. Valentino's story, about the kids with the puffin eggs. Now all the puffins were gone. Still, what other chance did we have?

"He's not looking as good as he was when we started the trip," I admitted to Simon.

"None of us are," said Juliette, scratching an arm.

Simon literally stroked his chin. "We need to let him adjust to the water temperature first," he said. "Why don't we put his aquarium in the shallows?"

I bent toward the pond and set the aquarium close to the shore so it was standing in an inch of water. Elvira leapt in the other direction and disappeared into the deep.

"Not exactly love at first sight, was it?" said Davy.

"She'll be back," Delph and I said at the same time.

"She'll be back," agreed Simon. I wasn't sure if we were going to be friends or not. But like Leroy, he was going to be a partner.

“How long do you think it will take?” asked Delphinium.

“We should let him adjust to the temperature for a half an hour at least,” Simon said.

“Right,” I said. “And then start adding some of the pond water to the aquarium so he doesn’t get water shock.” I wondered if that’s what had happened to the fish we saw in the Rehabilitation Center. Surely the government wouldn’t mess up something so simple. But they’d spent the past few decades saying the climate was fine. They were fighting with Canada. They *could* mess up something that simple. But we couldn’t. We’d brought Alph this far. We weren’t going to make any mistakes.

“Then what?” Juliette asked. “We just watch them the rest of the night?”

“Hold on a second,” Simon said. He turned and walked down a pathway that led to the normal part of his house. He came back a few minutes later.

“You should spend the night here,” he said. “We can set up sleeping bags and keep an eye on the frogs.”

“Yeah, except that our sleeping bags are all back at the campground,” Leroy said.

Simon’s mother walked into the room with a stack of clean, fluffy towels.

“Simon says you may be staying?” She placed the towels on one of the chairs. “I brought these in case you want to shower.”

Juliette's eyes brightened when she saw the towels. The idea of sleeping somewhere without mosquitoes was appealing, too.

"I could go get the stuff," Leroy volunteered.

"You can't carry it all," said Delph. "I'll go with you."

"I'll go, too," Davy said. At least Leroy and Delphinium wouldn't be alone together.

"Me too," said Juliette, her chaperone gene kicking in. "If I get first shower when we come back."

"Is it okay if I st—" I began.

"If you stay here and chaperone the frog date?" finished Leroy. "Knock yourself out."

"He won't even be out of the aquarium by the time you get back," I said.

Simon and I sat and looked at each other. At the half-hour mark, he went to the next room and returned with a beaker. He bent, awkwardly, and filled it partway with pond water. "May I?" he said.

"Of course."

Slowly, he got down on all fours. Then he reached out one of his arms and poured the water into the aquarium. When he was done, he backed away from the pond's edge. I was sure now that something was wrong with his legs.

"They're wired," he said.

"What?"

"My legs. That's the easiest way to describe it. Impulse

receptors. My brain tells them what to do and they do it; it just takes longer than most people."

"Have you always . . . ?" I wasn't sure how to finish the sentence.

"We were in a car accident when I was three," he said. "The control mechanism blipped out. My dad died. My legs sort of did, too, I guess. The technology's good, but it isn't perfect."

"So you just have to think about the movement and you move?"

"I don't even have to think that hard—it's almost like you, when your brain tells your body to walk across the room. Almost."

"Does it hurt?" I said.

"Yes and no," he said. "I feel pain. The doctors say I shouldn't, but I do."

"I'm sorry," I said.

"We should take out some water before we add more," he said.

I dipped the beaker—real glass—into the tank, retrieved some of the water, and set it aside—Simon wasn't sure about mixing new water into his pond, and this way, I could save it for later, to make the transition easier when we brought Alph back to the island.

Simon handed me another beaker, and I filled it, pouring the water into the tank. Alph moved to sit underneath the flow, so the water was sliding down his back. He was definitely perking up. He was going to be psyched when he saw that waterfall.

"I love sleeping in this room," Simon said. "I hardly ever get to. It feels just like camping, I'll bet."

"Have you ever been camping?" I'd never been myself before this week. I thought about the mosquitoes and the hungry deer.

Simon shook his head. "I'm sensitive to something in the air. If I spend too much time outside, I get sick."

"Then where'd you find Elvira?"

"Same place I found out about your frog," he said. "The Othernet. I'm on there a lot. It's . . . a way to get out. And break the rules."

I thought about Davy, a rule follower in real life but not in his virtual one.

"How long did it take you to do all this?"

"My whole life. My dad started it, before he died, with those two trees. He said he wanted to feel like he was outside all the time. My mom kept it up, as a tribute to him, mostly, but also because it was hard for me to get out. It was almost like my dad knew, she said. And then, when I got old enough, I started adding things. I've read about your government labs."

I made a face.

"Ours are better," he said. "But I thought I could do better than that even. I used to just have plants, but I started adding fish and birds." I wondered if the Disciples knew about Simon. Even if his dad had helped him start things, he'd done a lot. What did I have? A half-built CarbonClean and a bunch of other projects I'd started but hadn't finished. Simon had built an entire world.

I took some more water out of Alph's tank. Simon replaced it with pond water.

Alph was looking good now, alert, with his front feet clinging to the walls of the tank. There was a knock on the front door and Mrs. Laffitte opened it for Delph, Davy, Leroy, and Juliette, who were all lugging as much of our stuff as they could carry.

Mrs. Laffitte smiled at them, broadly this time. Maybe it was because Simon was smiling, too.

"Can we have s'mores?" he asked her. "Like real camping?"

"You already had cookies," she said.

"And hot dogs," Simon said. "On the range?"

"Simon, it's eleven o'clock." But I knew we were getting dogs and s'mores.

Juliette took her towel and headed for the shower while the rest of us set up sleeping bags on a grassy spot near the pond. Simon's mother came in with a sleeping bag for him, too, with a pad that went underneath. She rolled it out on the ground.

We waited until Juliette came back—the Lafittes had a CarbonClean, so it was more than two minutes—to let

Alph loose. By now, he was trying to get out of the aquarium and he looked as healthy as he had the first time we saw him.

"You can have the honors," I told Simon.

He lifted the screen and tipped Alph's tank—not far enough for the water to spill out, but enough so that the side of the tank was more like a slanted floor than a wall. Alph froze, like the animal statues at the Rehabilitation Center, but only for a second. He took a small hop to the lip of the tank and froze again. Hop. He made it to a rock this time. Finally, he took a real jump, extending his back legs, which were longer than I'd imagined, like when you take a metal spring and pull on both ends. He hit the water with a bloop and disappeared into Simon's pond.

"'One giant leap for mankind,'" Davy said. He was quoting from the first moon landing. "That's us."

"We're not leaping," I said. "The frog is."

"We're doing something," said Davy.

"Hopping," I said. "One small hop."

Davy shrugged. "It's still something," he said.

CHAPTER 21

"Let the date night begin," Juliette said. The allergy pills had kicked in and the bumps on her arms weren't as swollen, so it was easier to tell where one bite ended and the next one began. I was going to say she was in a better mood because of this, but actually, she'd been in a better mood ever since we'd crossed into Canada. Maybe the Canadian air agreed with her. Maybe she finally felt good about chaperoning a frog.

Simon's mom brought out the hot dogs, pink protein logs that we ate on buns, covered with condiments.

"*Fabas indulcet fames,*" Davy said. He didn't wait for Leroy to ask before he translated: "Hunger sweetens the beans."

The s'mores were good, too. The marshmallow goo was perfectly toasted and sticky. The chocolate was perfectly melted.

"Canadian chocolate," Simon said.

We decided to dim the lights so the bullfrogs would know it was night, and time for their hot date.

I got into my sleeping bag, between Delphinium's and Simon's.

We talked about dumb stuff, like school (Simon's was low residency, like Juliette's future college, instead of half residency, like ours) and the EPB (Canada's version of the EPF). That reminded Davy of Derek, and that led us back to the story of Leroy and the lobster.

"Can we *not* talk about that?" Leroy said.

"If the lobster had lived," Simon said, "they would have killed it eventually. Your EPF."

That didn't make Leroy feel any better.

"If he'd lived, they would have tried harder to figure out where he came from," Davy said. "They could have found the island and everything on it. When it died, they stopped caring."

I hadn't thought of it that way before. "Your lobster led us to Alph," I said. For some reason, I wanted Leroy to feel better, too. Besides, it was true.

"You know what's weird?" Delphinium said. "We wouldn't even be in this room if the lobster hadn't died. If you hadn't had the bucket."

We were all quiet, thinking about that, I guess.

"Why *did* you have the bucket?" I asked. "Did you know you'd find something?"

"Honestly?" Leroy said. "I wasn't sure the *Swan* would float. I brought the bucket in case I had to bail."

"You made a boat," Simon said. "You found your own island. Like the Galapagos."

"Like this room," Davy said. "This room is an island."

ERRRRRRRRRRRRRR.

The broken motor sound came from the pond.

ERRRR?

We let Alph croak as loud as he wanted. I got chills on my arms, even inside my sleeping bag.

"I wonder how long he's been calling like that, waiting for someone to answer?" Delph said. "And then he comes to a strange place and, all of a sudden, he isn't alone anymore." She paused. "I might cry." Which made me like her even more.

"Now that," whispered Juliette, "is true romance." Which made me like my sister a little more, too.

We heard a small splash. I imagined the frogs swimming toward each other in slow motion while violins and cellos played in the background.

"*Carpe noctem,*" Davy said.

"Is that Latin for 'get a room'?" asked Leroy.

"'Seize the night,'" Davy told him, at the same time Delph said, "Don't ruin the moment."

"We could serenade them," Davy said. I'd heard Davy sing enough to know this would not be enhancing the moment.

"In Latin?" Leroy asked.

"I'm in love with yooouuuu," Davy began. He was giddy. We all were. *"A love that's true and bluuueeee."*

"Green," I said.

"What?"

"A love that's true and green. Because they're frogs."

But I joined in on another chorus. Even Juliette did.

Above us, through the ceiling, we could see the stars again. There weren't as many as we saw from the woods—maybe because of the glass, or because we were in a town now and there was more light pollution—but we could see them just the same.

I could hear my friends' breath getting heavier and sleepier, but I didn't feel tired. I just lay there, listening to the sounds of the fans and the frogs.

"Ahab?" Delphinium whispered.

"Yeah," I said.

"Are you awake?"

"Well, yeah," I said. That made two of us; two of us awake in Simon's utopia. Frogtopia.

"Is this going to make a difference?"

There are three things you can do when the girl you like asks you a deep question in the middle of the night and you don't know the answer:

(A) turn it into a joke,

(B) answer truthfully, or

(C) ask her a philosophical question back, thus avoiding her question but letting her know you're taking her seriously.

I wanted to answer B, but the truth was, maybe Alph and Elvira would forget how to mate, and all this would have been for nothing. The truth was, even if they did figure out what to do, we could be raising a bunch of tadpoles who'd die one by one, like the puffins. The truth was, Elvira could lay eggs that wouldn't even hatch.

But maybe they would. And that was part of answer B, too. "I hope so," I told Delphinium. "Look. Some people need to believe in the tooth fairy or that the government is taking care of us or that, deep down, all people are good. And some people need to believe they can help save the world. I need to believe that."

"Saving the world," she said. "Is that what we're doing?"

"I like that better than thinking we spent our whole spring break trying to send two amphibians on a date."

There was another splash from the pond. For a minute, with Delph next to me and the smell of real flowers in a room that seemed alive, and with Alph hanging out in a pond with his brand-new girlfriend, it felt like I *could* save the world. It felt like I could do anything.

CHAPTER 22

"Frog spawn!"

I shed my sleeping bag and ran to join Simon, who stood by the side of the pond. His arm raised over his head in victory.

I thought he might be messing with me, or maybe the places that sold fake dog poop sold fake frog spawn, too. But it wasn't fake. The frogs were in Elvira's favorite spot, hiding behind the waterfall. Alph was on Elvira's back, his arms around her like he was getting a piggyback ride. Only they weren't going anywhere. They weren't even moving, except Alph's throat, which went in and out.

Elvira was sitting on a mass of what looked like clear glue with tiny specks of black, like a mass of eyeballs.

Frog spawn. Based on the number of eggs, it looked like we could repopulate the entire planet. If they hatched.

"There must be hundreds," said Leroy.

"How long do they stay like that?" Delph asked. She meant the frogs.

"Could be days," said Simon. He'd done his homework, too.

"I would just like to state that if we don't get home by Friday, my mom will kill me," Davy said. Our parents, mostly because of Davy's mom, had basically given us just enough time to make it to Canada and back—unless we pedaled really fast.

"We just have to let . . . nature take its course," I said. That's an expression my mother always used, but it had never seemed like nature had been on a proper course. Until now.

"We should give them some privacy," Juliette said.

"Like they care," said Leroy. "Have you no shame?" he asked the frogs. He turned back to us. "See? They don't care."

"It really was love at first sight," Juliette said.

Simon's mom called us for breakfast. I was hoping it would taste like the s'mores, but it turned out to be soy-real, just like we had at home, except with a French name, so it sounded fancier. *Soja-vie!*

"Put the dishes in the sanitizer when you're done," Mrs. Laffitte said. "You can do your schoolwork later, Simon. I suppose there's math in counting frog's eggs."

Simon let us each pick a plum from his tree. They were small and purple and shaped like raindrops, the kind you draw when you're in elementary school. Delph took a bite and then sucked on it a while, to make the sweetness last.

We all did. Most of the fruit I'd eaten was either hard because it'd been engineered to repel bugs and fungus, or else it had been combined with the good parts of other fruit to create some sort of frankenfruit.

"Save the pit," Simon said.

"Will it grow?"

He shrugged. "I haven't had much luck," he said. "You might."

We spent the rest of the morning tooling around the living room.

Simon told me where he'd gotten some of his seeds—not off the black market, but a green one. He had a room in his cellar where he'd been saving his own seeds and freezing them each time a flower bloomed and died. He gave me some to take back, the purple flox for Juliette, the jewelweed that had exploded on Delph, and some actual delphinium seeds, the blue kind, with white stars in the center.

I thought we'd plant the other seeds in my lab and on the island, though I wasn't sure I should mess with whatever balance was going on there. Non-native plants could be dangerous—even if the native plants were gone. Maybe I could try our yard instead, where there was no balance. But it was one thing to try to plant things inside a controlled environment, like Simon's house. It was another to try to plant them in a world full of vigilante fungus. I liked to think we could do it, though. Maybe we'd start an institute with all the people who hadn't given up yet. Maybe we'd find a way to start over. Simon Laffitte seemed like he could make things happen. And we were in sync. At least, that's what I thought until he pulled me aside after lunch.

"I want to buy your frog," he said.

"I told you before, he's not for sale."

"Everything has a price," Simon said. "The trip out here was hard on him. What's going to happen on the trip home? What if he doesn't make it back? He found a friend here. A partner. Do you really want to separate them now?"

My affection for Simon washed away like water. "Well, what about Elvira? We could take her with us."

"Then they'd both die," Simon said. "Plus, you couldn't afford her. No offense." I didn't point out that every time someone says "No offense," they usually mean to be offensive. "Anyway, she's not for sale."

"Neither is Alph."

"I'll give you fifty thousand."

"Dollars?" How much money did this kid have?

Simon looked at me and blinked twice.

It wasn't my decision. Davy and Delph and Leroy had been with me when we found him. Leroy had helped me catch him. And it was Leroy's island. It was Leroy's boat.

"He'd be safe here. He'd be with Elvira. And you'd have fifty thousand dollars. Maybe you could buy another bullfrog."

"Where?" I said.

"You can take the frog spawn," he said. "Not all of

it—we should have it in two places to increase the odds of survival. But when the eggs hatch, you won't need to buy another frog. You'll have tons of them."

"If," I said.

"When."

Pause.

"You could come back and visit Alph any time you wanted," Simon said. "I don't get a lot of visitors."

I wonder why? I thought. He sounded like the host on *Let's Make a Deal*, the nation's longest-running game show, which started on actual television. Behind Door Number One, you get a fabulous prize. But if you pick the wrong door: a zonk. There was even a mathematical theory of probability based on the show. In my case, the zonk was a dead frog.

What if I took Alph all the way home in his aquarium, and he died on the way, either because he suffocated in my satchel or because he was heartsick that I'd ripped him away from the only other creature of his kind he'd ever met? My experiment would be dead. My frog would be dead. My chance of becoming one of Darwin's Disciples would be extinct. On the other hand, he'd made it here in good shape, hadn't he? Well, *okay* shape, anyway. He was Blue Harbor's last bullfrog. He belonged there. With us.

I was down to two choices:

(A) bring him home, or

(B) give him a new one.

Normally, I could figure out the most correct answer. This time, they both seemed right. They both seemed wrong, too.

The others seemed to know something was up. They were watching us from across the living room. Especially Leroy. "It's not just up to me," I told Simon. "Go ahead. Tell them. Make your proposal."

So he did.

Leroy did the math. "That's ten thousand dollars apiece."

"But he's not really for sale, is he?" Delphinium asked. She went over to get a better look at Alph, who was still with Elvira in a sea of frog spawn.

"It looks like phlegm," Davy said.

Alph let out a long, belchy sound. It's not like I had the ability to read the frog's emotions or anything, but it sounded happier than the desperate croaks he'd been making on the island.

In my brain, it had been simple: Sneak across the border, introduce the frogs, sneak back across the border, go home. If they managed to reproduce, great. If not, try the next thing. The next experiment. Another way to save the world.

"Fifty thousand dollars," Leroy said again.

Maybe it had never been simple. It was getting less simple by the second.

CHAPTER 23

We spent one more night with Simon so the frogs could be together. Delph and Juliette did most of the talking, mostly to make up for my silence.

"When we get home," Leroy said in the morning, "I'm moving to that island until I find a frog of my own. I'm a pro at camping now."

"Alph's the only one," I said. "That's the whole point."

"I'll find a frog and sell him on the black market."

"Green market," Davy reminded him.

"Green market. But I'm only selling him to good guys. Like us."

I looked again at the frogs, who were apart now, but who still sat, side by side, rulers of the pond. Were we the good guys? We may have been better than the government. But I wasn't feeling like a good guy. *Trust no one*, my dad had written. It felt like he was talking about me.

"Goodbye to romance," Juliette said as I sliced off a clump of frog spawn and put it in my aquarium. She'd voted on selling Alph to Simon, though not for mercenary reasons. Leroy voted to sell, too. Delph and Davy voted with me, though they didn't seem so sure about it.

I mixed some of Simon's pond water with the water from back home. Then I pulled on some protective boots so I wouldn't harm Simon's ecosystem, and waded to the waterfall. The spray hit my face as I reached down to grab Alph from the rock. Even through my gloves, he felt slimy, the healthy kind of slimy.

He looked at me, a long, sad look. I had a hard time deciding whether:

(A) I was imagining it,

(B) he was depressed about leaving, or

(C) he was hungry. (I'd caught some bugs in Simon's yard for the return trip, but I was saving them.)

Anyway, even if the answer was B, Alph wouldn't be alone for long. The tadpoles would hatch and turn into frogs.

Unless they didn't.

I waded back to the shore and settled Alph in the aquarium on top of the eggs. Then I loaded the aquarium into my dad's satchel. Alph let out a long, throaty croak. It sounded like a moan.

Silence again, except for the waterfall, where Elvira sat alone. I kept hearing words in the rush of the water—*don't-do-it* over and over and over.

"Oh, ALL RIGHT." I pulled the aquarium out of the satchel. "Keep him," I told Simon.

"Excellent."

"Wait, what happened to 'All of us are making this decision, we're partners'?" asked Leroy.

"It's the right thing," I said. Right for the frog. Just right.

"Who do you think voted to let him stay? Oh, wait, I remember: ME."

"For the money," I said.

He glared at me.

"It *is* the right thing," said Delph. She was standing directly behind me, so I could feel her words as well as hear them.

I wasn't going to be one of the youngest people ever initiated into Darwin's Disciples. That would be Simon, if they found out about him. Me? I was just going to be a kid who had caught a frog once. A kid who had caught a frog and let him go.

Juliette threw her arms out wide. "Hello to romance," she said.

I handed the aquarium to Simon. "Take good care of my frog," I said.

"Our frog," Leroy said. "Take good care of *our* frog."

I unpacked the screen pouch, where I'd put the bugs for the trip home. "Here," I said. "Give them this for a wedding present." It sounded angrier than I meant it to, given that this was supposed to be a big happily-ever-after.

"Remember, we get visitation rights," Juliette said. I stared at my sister. "What?" she said. "He's part mine, too."

"So about the money," Leroy said. "If he's keeping the frog . . ."

Delphinium gave him a look.

"He offered us a deal," Leroy said. "*A really good deal.*"

"It doesn't feel right. Taking the money," I said.

"Well, it feels right to me. I could *use* that money," Leroy said.

Simon turned toward Leroy. Slowly, he set the aquarium on the ground. "What if I gave you money in a different way?" he said. "Over time. A grant."

"A grant?"

"Like researchers get at universities."

"I'm not a researcher," Leroy said. "I'm a builder."

"What would we research?" I asked.

"Whatever you wanted," Simon said. "Frogs. Plants. You could buy tools and materials and set up a proper lab. I'll bet you could build your own greenhouse if you wanted to. You could do a lot, with money like that."

"The EPF has money like that. They aren't changing anything," Leroy said.

"The EPF isn't us," I said.

"Am I included in this 'us'?" Leroy asked.

"We're partners," I said.

Leroy stiffened a little. Maybe he *had* overheard me and Delphinium talking that time. "It's still not the same as a new bike," he said.

"Yeah. Well. Your old bike probably runs better than anything out there."

Leroy started to grin. "Yeah," he said.

"What else would you do with the money?" I asked. "A new wardrobe?"

He shrugged.

"You can buy your own hip waders," I offered.

"My own hip waders and I can build stuff?" he said.

I nodded.

So did he.

I looked at Simon. "Why?"

"You don't trust my altruism?" he asked. It was a Davy sort of word.

I shrugged.

"It's because I can," he said. "And will."

There were people all over the world who could but didn't. Simon could and did. Now he was offering to let us do something, too. Of course, he was also taking something away.

We got the rest of our stuff loaded.

"If we're not bringing Alph, should we put the frog spawn in something else?" Leroy asked.

"What do you mean?"

"To make it easier to sneak across," he said.

"Great idea," said Delphinium. How many great ideas could one person have? "What would we put it in?"

"A thermos," I said.

"Since we're not carrying live contraband," Delph said, "why do we have to sneak? We're frog free. Can't we just go back through a checkpoint? That way Davy's mom won't freak out if she's tracking us."

"We never checked in," Juliette said. "If they see five Americans leaving Canada but nothing that says we crossed over, won't they be suspicious? We might be better off sneaking back." I couldn't believe she was even suggesting it.

"We can tell him somebody forgot to fill in the paperwork," Leroy said. "Telling people things is my specialty."

"We can change the records," Davy said. "That's mine. I can find a back door. If Simon will let me tap into his network."

Sometimes it takes an awful lot of rule breaking to keep from breaking another rule. But Davy scanned our index fingers and went into Simon's bedroom. He came out thirty minutes later.

"Five Americans visiting Canada for spring break," he said. "We've been here since Monday morning, if anybody asks."

The spring break part wasn't even a lie.

We finally posed for our photo with Alph before we left. Simon took it. Delph thought Simon should be in it, too, so we took another on a timer with him and Elvira. I hoped someday it would have historical significance. I hoped it was the start of something. Simon let Elvira go back into the pond. Alph wriggled in my hands, eager to follow.

"Well," Leroy said. "I guess we'd better say goodbye to the last frog in Blue Harbor, Maine."

"Goodbye, Alph," Delphinium said. She air-kissed him, just above his forehead.

"Bye, big guy," said Leroy.

"Be a good dad," Davy said.

"Remember the right way to treat a lady," Juliette told him.

When I'd researched frogs, I'd learned a bit about their memories—enough to know they didn't really work like ours. "I'll always remember you, Alph," I said. He looked back at me with his amber eyes and I crouched down near the water. "Don't forget me," I whispered, and let him go.

Alph leapt out of my hands. His splash sent ripples everywhere.

I heard a few sniffles. Some of them were mine. I stood up. "He's not going to be the last one," I said. I grabbed the thermos of frog spawn and held it above my head, like I was the Statue of Liberty. We looked up at the thermos. It wasn't lit, but it was still a torch.

"I'll see you all soon," Simon said.

"Yeah," I told him. "You will."

CHAPTER 24

It didn't take long to reach the border, now that we were pros. Also, we were riding on main pikes instead of through the woods. I mostly trusted Davy's hacking skills, so I wasn't especially worried about making it across. Then I saw the sign, in English and French, about handing over all liquids for "review."

"I thought they only did that for air travel," Juliette said. "We're on *bikes*."

"They can do whatever they want," Davy said dismally.

"Darn it," I said, forgetting to substitute a science experiment. I'd given up Alph. I couldn't give up his progeny, too.

Ahead of us, the border patrol was opening car trunks and scanning them with a wand. I saw them take a bottle of what looked like just water and pour it onto the parched ground. They didn't even use it to water the plants.

"Let's go back," I said. "We can cross somewhere else."

But Leroy nodded his head toward the guards. "They're watching us," he said, without really moving his lips. "If we turn around and leave, they'll think we have something to hide."

"We *do* have something to hide," Davy said.

"We still have rights," said Juliette. "They need a warrant to search us."

Ahead of us, a guard was questioning a kid about half our age. The kid was crying. If the five of us turned around and left, would they let us go skipping off into the woods? I didn't think so.

"We need to find somewhere else to put the spawn," I said. "Somewhere that they won't dry out."

"My armpit?" Leroy asked.

"Your mouth," Davy said, in English, not Latin.

"That could work," I said. "A mouth is wet and it isn't chlorinated."

"That was a joke," Davy said.

"It *was* a joke," said Delph. "Now it's a solution. Well. A possible solution."

I expected Juliette to be grossed out. "It won't be the worst thing we've ever eaten," she said.

"Tasted," I said. "Don't swallow anything."

Delph pulled one of her barrettes out of her hair and handed it to me. "You can divide it with this," she said. "I'd do it in the bathroom."

The guards were still watching us. "Okay," I said. "Meet me by the bathroom door in five minutes."

I left my bike outside the restroom, which was white and bright, like a place you'd perform surgery instead of pee. I sat down in one of the stalls.

You weren't supposed to move frog spawn and we had. Splitting the spawn into bite-size chunks wasn't good, either. Frogs laid tons of eggs because so few made it to adulthood. Now I was the main environmental hazard threatening their survival. I plunged the sharp end of the barrette into the spawn. Davy was right: It was a little like phlegm.

Outside the bathroom, I handed out the pieces, hoping human spit wasn't too warm, wasn't another environmental hazard.

We decided Delphinium would keep her mouth spawn free, in case we needed to do some fast talking.

"After you, Good Influence," Leroy said as we wheeled our bikes toward the line for pedestrians. He sounded the way Juliette did when she had her wisdom teeth pulled.

Juliette insisted on going first, since she was the chaperone. She put her finger in front of the scanner as a guard took her bike and waved a wand around it. I wasn't sure what they were scanning for.

Another guard did the questioning. "Reason for visit?"

"Pleasure," Juliette said, moving only half her mouth.

"A tourist?"

"Yes."

The guard nodded her through. When I saw her breathe, I realized it was because before that, she hadn't been breathing. I couldn't believe she'd gotten through so easily. They didn't even dump out any of her hair stuff. Delph and Davy went through next, with no problem.

"You." A guard was nodding toward Leroy. "Come through this line."

We exchanged glances as I stepped ahead in my own line and put my finger on the scanner.

"Name?" the guard asked. He hadn't asked any of the others. It was right there, in the scan.

"Jonathan Goldstein." I worked hard to keep my voice normal.

"Destination?"

"Home."

"Reason for visiting Canada?"

"Pleasure." That's what Juliette had said. "And, um, recreation. We were camping."

"Why would you want to do that?" he said.

I tried to channel Leroy. "Why not?" I said.

"We have plenty of beautiful spots here in the United States," he said. "When did you arrive?"

"Monday," I told him.

"Time?"

What time had Davy put in there? "I don't remember the time."

"I am obligated to remind you that it is against the law

to transport any agricultural products across the border, including produce. Do you have anything to declare?"

"No," I said.

"No alcohol or firearms?"

"No."

"Did you at any time during your international vacation talk to any person or persons wishing to harm the United States or its government?"

"What? No."

He waved a wand over my backpack. Then he looked through it with a small baton. He used it to hold up a pair of my underwear. I hoped Delph was looking in the other direction. Ahead of me, another guard was unzipping the satchel on my bike. I almost smiled, and would have, if I hadn't been afraid of squishing the frog spawn: The aquarium had stayed in Wodiska Falls.

"What's this?" The guard lifted my thermos, which I'd reattached to my bicycle.

"A thermos."

"What's in it?"

"Water," I told him. Which was true. I'd left the remainder of the pond water there so that we'd have a place to stow the frog spawn when we got across.

The guard poured some of the water out of the thermos.

"We're biking," I said. "I need that water." I didn't see any drinking fountains. Not that the water would have been safe for the spawn, even if I had.

"You can purchase new water at the rest stop up ahead," he said. He handed me my empty thermos. "Welcome home."

I walked toward the others. Leroy finally cleared customs, too, and followed me. None of us said anything.

"He dumped my water," I said through one side of my mouth as we walked our bikes toward the pike. Above us, drones flitted around like mosquitoes. I wasn't sure if they were looking or listening. We rode out of view of the border, but a few of the drones were still overhead. We stopped, and Delph reached into her satchel and pulled out the umbrella she'd taken with us on our trip out to the island, the one that was supposed to make us look like a painting.

"Brilliant." I spit the frog spawn back into the thermos and then passed it around so the others could, too. I didn't see the rest stop yet. And we had no water to add.

"Maybe this will help," said Delph. She pulled a small vial of water from her satchel. "It's from Simon's pond," she said. "In case of emergencies."

"How did they not see that?" Leroy asked incredulously. He held up his own test tube, but it was empty, as was his thermos of drinking water. They'd dumped them both at the crossing.

Delph added her water to the thermos. It only covered up the eggs about halfway.

"Any other ideas?" I said.

"Spit," Delph said. It was the softball player in her. I found this very attractive.

I checked my One to see if anyone had conducted an experiment on the effects of human saliva on frog spawn. All I found was research on frog saliva, which wasn't the same.

"We could use pee," said Leroy. "It's supposed to be more sterile."

I wasn't sure who made him chief scientist. "Pee could give them ammonia poisoning," I said. "Spit's better. And they've already been exposed to it anyway."

"Okay, then," Leroy said. And he spit a mouthful of saliva into the thermos.

We passed it around, spitting, until our mouths were dry and the top of the frog spawn was covered.

Juliette pulled out some of the water we'd refilled from Simon's—from his sink, not his pond. She took a sip, and then passed that around, too, trying to recover.

"Sneaking across worked better," Juliette said. "We'll have to remember, for next time."

I still couldn't believe my sister was thinking about a next time—or that she'd sneak back across, especially when the thought of it had almost derailed our whole trip. I took another sip of water and handed back the thermos. We'd made it across the border. Now it would be smooth sailing (or pedaling) all the way home.

CHAPTER 25

There are certain things you shouldn't think or say out loud. "Smooth sailing" is one of them. Because that's a sure way to make something bad happen.

The first thing happened just past the checkpoint, when we were crossing the bridge back into Maine. Davy stopped to take a picture and set his One up on the railing. But he hadn't gotten off his bike to do it, and his handlebars turned at the last second. They knocked into the One, sending it over the side and into the river below.

"Nooo!" he yelled. He started to mourn before we even knew if the One was dead. The river was moving fast, swollen from a sudden rain. When we reached the end of the bridge, we left our bikes and scrambled down along the bank, going from rock to rock to get closer to where it had fallen. All we saw was water, foggy with mud.

All his codes and keys—gone. Also: "She's going to kill me," he said.

Two minutes later, Mrs. Hudson's face bloomed out of

my One. That's how we knew for sure that Davy's One was dead.

"Davy's dot is missing," she said. She'd been tracking him, the way we'd been tracking Alph, but with his One instead of a chip and some Bind-oh.

"It fell," I said. "Uh, I'm not sure he can talk. He's pretty upset."

Mrs. Hudson knitted her eyebrows together and I turned my One around so she could see Davy, who was looking out at the water so we couldn't see him tearing up.

"Davy. Child, look at me. Are you all right?"

He gave her a thumbs-up sign, even though we all knew he was feeling thumbs-down—worse, now that she'd called him "child" in front of us.

"Where did you drop it?"

Davy didn't answer. I turned the One so that her flickering face was staring out at the river. "There."

"What are you doing in that water?"

"We're not in it, just near it. We were up there." I showed her the bridge.

Then she gave us a lesson on engineering, and the danger of bridges. I don't know how else she thought we were going to get from one place to another. I tried to explain that the trail included the bridge, but she didn't listen.

"I'll be keeping your number, Jonathan," she told me, using my real name. "I'll be in touch."

Great. Now I had inherited Mrs. Hudson. Davy didn't turn away from the water until she was gone. We searched a little longer, putting all our Ones on search and scan, but we didn't turn up anything. Finally, we slogged back up the hill.

We didn't have as much energy as before. Maybe we were pedaling slower, without Alph's croaks to urge us on. The sun began to set before we reached the certified campground, so we pulled off in a small wooded area. Leroy collected dead wood for a fire and put stones around it to keep it contained. The stew was nearly boiling when Mrs. Hudson popped out of my One to check on Davy, who still wasn't saying much. Delphinium used her own One to check in with her parents. We put the Ones away after that so Davy wouldn't feel as bad about his loss. If we hadn't, we might have been quicker about setting up the tents. If we hadn't, we might have heard the warning.

The first we saw of the storm was the dark clouds that blotted out the last traces of the sunset. The sky went from hot pink to a sickish green, before fading to black. The temperature dropped. The air buzzed with electricity.

"That is one ticked-off sky," Leroy said.

Juliette pulled her One out of her pocket again, but it was as dark as the sky. "Engage," she said. It didn't. None of them did.

Delph's eyes got wide as the sky rumbled and the rain came. Steady sheets. We stood under a tree as hail interrupted the rain and then the rain returned. It hit the ground so hard and so fast that it pooled up, as if the trees weren't even thirsty. Our fire dissolved into water and ash. The stew-pot filled with rain and sloshed over the sides.

Thunder again. Loud. A tree limb crashed to the ground. We barely heard it, but we felt it.

"This is not the safest place to be during a thunder-storm," I said.

"It can't last long, hard as it's coming," Juliette said. "We should shelter in place."

That's what they had us do in school when a weather event was coming.

Leroy grabbed our tent and set it up like he was trying to win a world record. I wasn't sure it counted as shelter, but we all scooted through the flap.

"You were right," Juliette said, wrinkling her nose. "About the smell."

"Dad's feet," I said. It was worse in the rain.

The tent was supposed to be waterproof, but water still seeped through the top and the bottom.

"Put the Ones in here," Leroy said, pulling out a container.

Thunder exploded around us. I counted the seconds between the lightning and the thunder and divided by three to account for the speed of sound—a kilometer every three seconds. The storm wasn't getting farther away. It was getting closer.

Outside we heard the *plink* of more hail bouncing off our bicycles, which were pressed up next to a tree.

The frog spawn was still in the satchel. And okay, the satchel was probably as good a protection as the tent was, and the thermos was hard and metal. But I couldn't leave it out there.

I unzipped the tent.

Juliette opened her mouth, but she must have realized right away what I wanted to get. She knew she wasn't going to stop me.

BOOM.

I waited until the next lightning flash, then bolted toward the bikes. I opened the satchel and grabbed my thermos.

"Two one thousand." I was ready for the thunder when it came.

Then lightning split the sky. I heard a crack and then the rain, the hail, all of it disappeared.

I opened my eyes, but I didn't remember closing them. I saw the blue of the tent, smelled the smell of dirty feet. I didn't remember running back there. I felt a squeeze and looked at my hand. Delphinium was holding it, a good indication that I was dreaming.

"Hey, you're awake." Leroy's voice had an echoey quality to it.

"Jonathan, you jerk." Juliette sounded pissed, but she looked puffy, like she'd been crying. Over me?

"Why?" My voice sounded like my mouth was full of gauze from the emergency kit. Something hurt. My head.

My arm. My ankle. I smelled something burning, but it wasn't just the drowned campfire. It smelled like the first explosion I'd made with my chemistry set, or the way the Soov smelled when my dad started it up.

Delphinium squeezed my hand again. I hoped my fingers didn't feel too sweaty.

"Did we get struck by lightning?" I said. Maybe it had altered our electrical structure and we were turning into superheroes. Frog Boy. Climate Girl.

"Not *we*," Leroy said. "*You*."

"Transitive property," said Davy. "You got struck by a tree. The tree got struck by lightning."

"Where are the eggs?" The gauzy feeling was going away. A panicky feeling replaced it.

Leroy held up my thermos. There was a dent in it, but I didn't see any cracks.

"Are the bikes okay?"

"They were," Leroy said. "I can check. The rain's let up."

"For now," said Juliette as Leroy scooted out of the tent.

"How did you get the tree off me?" I looked through the tent flap, toward Leroy, but Davy pointed to Delphinium. "It was mostly her," he said.

Delph let go of my hand and made a muscle. "Pitching arm," she said. So she was the superhero. I could live with that.

"You can't ride a bike like that." Davy looked at me like

I was his fallen commander. Juliette stood up like she'd received a battleground promotion.

"I'm going for help."

"We should stick together." Leroy was back, his hair plastered to his face. He didn't offer a report. I wasn't sure if that was a good sign or a bad one.

"I'm going," said Juliette. "The storm's over."

"*For now.* Those were your words," Leroy told her. "Aren't there lines of storms?"

Pain spiked through my ankle and up my leg before I could agree. My face must have shown it. That was why Davy said I couldn't make it. His face looked like it had the day he came to see me, after we'd made the bet, and my mom had said I was too sick to come out. I'd watched him through the window and wished I wasn't sick, and it wasn't because I wanted to be better. It was because of Davy's face.

"Here." Delph handed me a small yellow pill.

"Thanks, Doc," I said. I turned my head and that's when I saw my arm. There was a towel over it, but through the towel, I could see red. I'd cut myself before, enough to get down to the fat and muscle, though not the bone. It didn't hurt now. But it looked like it should have hurt. A lot.

"Holy—"

"We think you sliced it on a rock when you fell," Davy said, looking away. "That's the working hypothesis."

Hypothesis sounded better than *giant gash.* The word calmed me down.

The thunder blasted, loud again, and the wind attacked our tent. If we weren't in there weighting it down, it would have blown away.

"See?" Leroy said.

"So maybe I'll stay a few more minutes," Juliette said. She opened the container, tried to turn on her One, and put it back. The thunder came again, in a roll this time, instead of a bang.

"*Who cares if it's raining?*" Juliette started singing. My mother sang that song when we were kids. "*Who cares if it's blue? Who cares if it's raining? I want to dance with you.*" The song's about a guy who doesn't care that it's raining (obviously) because he's finally found true love. Juliette usually has a good voice, but now she was singing loud and off-key, maybe so no one would feel bad about joining in. Well, no one but Davy, who registered a meteorological objection.

"If the sky was blue, it wouldn't have been raining," he said. "The sky would have been gray. Or green."

"Metaphor." Leroy shrugged and went back to singing. "*Who cares if it's storming? There's sunshine in your eyes. You came without a warning and blew clouds from the skies.*"

The thunder came again. Juliette didn't remember the third verse, so she sang the first one again. The third time through, no one joined in and we went back to listening to the storm.

"Nice weather for frogs," Delph said. Now *she* pulled

out the Ones to see if any of them flickered. I wondered what my frog—Simon's frog—was doing at Simon's. How many storms like this had he survived? Delphinium must have known I was thinking about him, because the next thing she said was "You know, maybe we should just name the island after Alph."

"Second the motion," said Davy.

I could get behind that, too. Even though it hurt to do it, I nodded.

CHAPTER 26

The rain pounded the earth, too much, too soon. We could hear the trees, their roots ripping up soggy ground as they fell. We heard the squall of the wind.

Then we heard another sound. Not the falling of a tree or the croaking of a bullfrog. It was louder and steadier. There was a blinding light.

"I'll check it out," Juliette said.

"Me too." Leroy stood up, as much as he could in the tent. "You copes?"

"Oh, sure," I said. "Don't mind me. I'll just wait here."

I wasn't copes. What I was, was useless. *What did you do over spring break?* I imagined the prompt from my English teacher. And what *had* I done? Gone to Canada with my friends and Leroy. What did I have to show for it? I hadn't saved the world. I didn't have a frog, I'd broken a few bones, probably, and I'd stranded my friends in the middle of a storm.

Juliette screamed, shaking me out of my pity party. But it wasn't a scream of horror.

"It's Dad," she said. "And he's got the Soov."

The motorized, gasoline-powered, emissions-belching Soov was here, in the middle of the woods. This was the first time I'd known it to be anywhere but in our garage or the July Fourth parade. You could tell that my dad didn't drive it much. From my spot in the tent, I could see the headlights zipping back and forth, getting closer. I could hear brakes and the quiet when the engine stopped and Juliette's voice talking over the rain. Leroy moved the tent flap, and the headlights filled our tent with blinding brightness. Then they turned off, too.

"How did you even know to look for us?" Juliette said as the others filed out of the tent.

"Davy's mom. When she couldn't reach you, she called me. I'd seen the weather report and thought I'd drive out here. Save Kim from a heart attack."

"Are we going back in the Soov?" That was Davy.

"This car," said my dad, "was the only thing big enough to fit all of you. What was I going to drive? The Piquant?" I pictured the hydro we shared with our neighbors. Pro: It could drive itself. Con: It would have only fit three of us. "Anyway, who's going to be out on a night like this to see me drive it?" He paused. "And where the hell is Ahab?"

"Here." I waved my good arm through the tent flap.

"There was an accident," Juliette said. He didn't wait for her to finish. I heard the Soov door open and a pair of feet sloshing through the mud. The tent flap lifted and my father's round face appeared. He scanned me up and down, methodically, the way scientists do when they're watching for a deviation in their results.

"Arm?" he said.

"And ankle."

"Can you put any weight on it?" I tried to wiggle it. Bad idea; pain raced through my leg.

I shook my head, wondering why it hurt so much when it was other parts of me that felt broken. "And head," I added.

He bent down and lifted the towel that was covering the bleeding part of my arm. Then he put it back and looked away. "I've seen worse," he said, but he didn't sound convincing. "Let's pull that on a little tighter." He wrapped the towel around me so I could feel the pressure. Then he reached down and scooped me up. Pain raced through my ankle when it moved. I saw light, but it wasn't from the car. "Easy," my dad said. "Easy." He put me in the back seat of the Soov. My wet clothes stuck to the seat.

"Pack it up, kids," he said.

He did not mean me. My friends packed up our gear and loaded it into the Soov while I lay splayed out in the back. He was right: There was room inside for all of us. The Soov even had an attachment for our bikes.

Juliette took the passenger seat. Davy, Leroy, and Delph sat in the wayback, leaving me the whole middle to myself and my ankle, which felt like it was on fire.

"One of you help Ahab," my dad said. Between the two

front seats, I could see the silhouette of his face. I thought about Derek and his dad, carbon copies of each other. My dad and I were nothing alike—not our hair, not our height, not our ideas about the universe. He'd never saved the world. But he might have tried once. And he'd come north to save me.

Juliette leaned over and pulled a strappy thing down from the top of the seat and clicked it at the bottom. Apparently, it was supposed to go over one shoulder, instead of both like the harness in the hydro. Because I was lying down, Juliette strapped it over my hip. I held on to the thermos like it was the blue teddy bear I'd had when I was little, before I knew that real bears had never come in that color, before I knew that real bears were in trouble. My dad turned the ignition key and pressed down on the pedal to move the car backward. We jerked. Even harnessed in, I nearly rolled off the seat. We jerked again as my dad switched gears. He turned the Soov right and then too far left.

"It just takes a little getting used to," said my dad. "Practice." He didn't get any driving practice with the hydro. And Fourth of July came just once a year.

My dad swerved again. There was a bump and the Soov stopped moving. He gunned the gas, and the engine roared. I could hear a tire spin.

"Is it broken?" asked Davy.

"Stuck." My dad slammed his hands against the steering wheel. "Okay, plan B. Jules, you sit behind the wheel.

Everyone else, come push." They all bailed out. Again, he did not mean me.

"One, two, three," he yelled. On "three," Juliette pushed the gas, a little timidly.

"Gun it, Jules. One, two, three."

She pushed harder. I could hear it in the engine.

I could also hear Delphinium saying "stroke, stroke," and Leroy laughing. And then:

"We could use this branch," Leroy said. "For traction."

Ka-ching. Another great idea for Leroy.

"Grab a bunch," I yelled.

Only Juliette was there to hear me. "What?" she said.

"Tell them to break down a bunch of sticks. Fill the hole." She passed along the message.

I heard a crunching sound and the Soov lumbered forward slowly. Juliette screamed and slammed on the brakes. "Now move it into 'park,'" my dad said. "Where the P is."

She looked relieved when my dad switched places with her, and even more relieved when we finally reached the highway and the ride smoothed out. The rain had slowed some, but it was still hard to see. The windshield wipers shrieked back and forth. There were no other lights. We were the only ones on the road.

"How's it feel, champ?" my dad asked. "Do we find the nearest hospital?"

My arm was cut deep, but with the towel pulled tight, the blood didn't seem to be a problem. My ankle was still on fire. Delphinium didn't seem as interested in injuries related to blood as she had been in rashes, but she leaned over the seat and looked at my face. "Well?"

"I can wait until Blue Harbor General," I said. I figured Mrs. Hudson would freak if it took us much longer to get home. And I wanted to get the frog spawn into a proper tank as soon as possible.

While my dad drove, Juliette told him about our trip. She even mentioned Alph. "You have to swear not to tell," she said.

"Like you did," mumbled Leroy.

"A real frog?" said my father. "No kidding." For once, he didn't mention anything about his childhood. And she didn't mention that we'd snuck across the border. My sudden coughing fit stopped her from saying anything about the eggs.

"We really liked Valentino's," she said.

"Best ice cream ever."

"It's not real ice cream anymore," Juliette said.

"Figures."

"You never told us you were in Canada for an environmental conference," I said from the back.

"I didn't?" I could see him shrug in the darkness. "I must have forgotten that part." *The most important part.*

He whistled a little bit as he steered toward home. He stopped when we neared Blue Harbor.

"Crap," he said.

Even from lying down in my seat, I could see the reflection of the blue lights.

"What's happening?" I asked.

"There's a sinkhole," said Delph. "It's taken out half the road. The EPF is here . . . and Officer Ripley."

I guessed a sinkhole was considered "environmental." My dad rolled down the window.

"Ted," said Officer Ripley. "What a surprise. I'll need to see your license and registration."

"Look, it was an emergency," my dad said.

"Out of the car," said Officer Ripley.

My dad cut the motor and slid out of the driver's seat. He tried laughing it off again. "Angus, you know I wouldn't drive this thing if I didn't have to. Have I ever done it before?"

Officer Ripley didn't laugh.

"Ahab," Davy whispered. "He's got a dog."

That wasn't good.

"And he's got Derek."

I needed to think, but the pain made it hard to concentrate. "We have to get the frog spawn out of here. If the dog . . ." I didn't know if EPF dogs were trained to sniff for frog spawn, but I knew they were trained to find things that were out of the ordinary. Frog spawn was out of the ordinary.

"Can you get to the bikes?" I asked.

"Yes," said Juliette. "Some of them."

"Okay, here's the strategy." I felt like a coach. "Davy: Get on a bike and ask if you can go home because your mother is going to be worried. Anybody who knows you can confirm that."

"I got you."

"While Davy's talking to Officer Ripley, Leroy will take another bike and head to my shed with the frog spawn."

"What if I kill it?" Leroy said. "Or drop it?"

"I already dropped it," I said.

"Check, then," Leroy said. "What if Derek follows me?"

"You'll figure it out."

"What if they ask where we've been?"

"Say we were visiting a friend," I said. It didn't feel like the truth yet. But it felt like someday it might be.

CHAPTER 27

"Look," my dad was telling Derek's dad. "I don't have time for this. I have to get my kid to the hospital. And you don't have time for this, either. You've got to deal with this hole."

"Mr. Goldstein," said Davy. His voice was high and whiny. Perfect pitch.

"What, Davy?"

"My mom's going to be climbing the walls if she doesn't hear from me."

"She's already climbing the walls," my dad said. To Officer Ripley, he said: "His mom is Kim Hudson."

"I'll let her know you're safe," Officer Ripley said.

"Come on, Angus. Just let him go. The kid wasn't driving this thing. I was."

"She really needs to see me in person," Davy said, removing the bike from the back of the Soov. I could hear his voice getting a little farther away. "If she doesn't, she'll get really upset."

"Kid," Mr. Ripley yelled. "Come back here. Now, where's that one going?" And I knew Leroy had taken off in the other direction.

"Hey," Derek said. "That's Varney."

Go, Leroy.

"The Lobster Killer," Derek said. "I'll bring him in for questioning."

"Would you mind telling me where you were?" Officer Ripley said.

"I found them at a campground in Beulah," my dad said. "The storm cut off our communication and I went to find them in case something happened. As you can see from my son's bleeding arm and broken ankle, something happened."

"I'm going to have to check the car," said Officer Ripley.

"For what?" asked my dad. "Wet socks? They're in there."

I lifted myself up to see the sinkhole through the windshield, gaping, like the earth had opened its mouth and wanted to swallow us. Revenge, maybe, for all we'd done to it. I didn't know what Officer Ripley could do about the hole. Maybe that's why he was focusing on us: My dad seemed like something he could control.

"Infractions," said Officer Ripley as I sank back down onto the seat. "I'm sworn to protect the world from people like you."

Blindly, I thought. Without seeing the forest. Without even seeing the trees.

"The whole vehicle is an infraction," said my dad. "A rolling infraction. I'm guilty as charged. I get it. I'll pay. But would you please let me get my kid to the hospital?"

"Where does she think she's going?" Delph must have taken off, too.

"Maybe she didn't like my driving," my dad said. "Look, if you were a kid, would you rather go home on a functional bicycle or spend three hours with me in a hospital waiting room?"

"Dad," I called from the car. It wasn't a fake diversion. The pain in my ankle made everything around me look red. My face was clammy with either new sweat or old rain. I guess I must have been pretty pale, because when Officer Ripley looked in the back seat, he said, "Even if this is an emergency, you've broken about seventeen laws by driving this thing."

"Fine," my dad said. "Charge me. Look, I messed up, Angus, I get it. But you have to know I wouldn't drive this thing unless I had to. Look at him."

I lifted my head off the sticky car seat and tried to look as pathetic as possible. It wasn't a stretch.

Mr. Ripley nodded, just once. "But this isn't over," he said.

"Fine," said my dad. On the seat beside him was another green slip. I was betting there was a check mark next to every box on there.

Juliette took another bike and went home to be with Mom while my dad took me to the hospital. He couldn't seem to sit properly in the chair, but he didn't look away when they cut open my jeans to examine my ankle. He didn't look away when they cleaned up my arm, either. They gave me a shot to numb it first. That hurt worse than the sealant they used to glue the skin together. Not knowing what had happened to the eggs hurt most of all.

They gave me a pair of scrubs and a pair of crutches, but I leaned on my dad to get back to the car. He settled me in the back again, though I sat up this time, with my leg stretched out across the seat.

"The original Ahab lost part of his leg," my dad said. "I'm glad you got to keep yours." From looking at his face, I could tell he'd actually been worried about that.

He slammed the door and got in the front seat.

"Dad?" I said. He didn't answer, but he looked back over his shoulder to show that he'd heard me.

"What happened after Canada? After your trip, I mean."

"I came home," he said.

That part was obvious. "Did you get arrested?" I said. "Did you stay friends with the Mellor twins? Did you earn your Planet Protection badges?"

"Now, how did you know about that?"

"Your journal was in the satchel," I said. "You left a lot of pages blank."

"I wasn't much of a writer," he said. "Let's see. The Mellor twins moved, and we didn't keep in touch, though I did hear that Chris became a lawyer. In the Planet Protectors, I made it as far as Earth Warrior. And as for jail, the answer is no, I didn't go. We got thrown in the back of a police car and they scared us a little. Told us to go make some signs and stand in front of our own capitol. They said that's where the change needed to happen."

"Did you?"

"A couple of times."

"How come you gave up?"

"We didn't want to go to jail," he said.

"Not on the conference. On saving the world."

My dad turned to the front again, so I couldn't see his face. "We just didn't get anywhere, Ahab," he said. "It felt like no matter what we did, nothing changed. The president never read petitions—anyone's, not just ours. He didn't care. I guess, after a while, it seemed easier to let somebody else fix things. And a while after that, I let myself be convinced that less needed fixing than I thought."

I'd never heard my dad be that honest. But it didn't make me feel better.

"You were lazy," I said.

"Yes," he agreed. "There's nothing easier than denial."

But that wasn't true. Denial seemed like something he had to work at. My mother, too.

My dad turned the key in the ignition. When he spoke again, his voice was quiet.

"Maybe I didn't give up completely. I had you, didn't I?" He coughed like he'd swallowed wrong, and put the Soov into drive. We headed home.

Everyone was waiting in the kitchen: my friends, their parents, my sister. They cheered when I hobbled into the kitchen. I thought about Simon, and the way he had to think every time he took a step. I'd have to do that, too, but only for about eight weeks. I searched my friends' faces for a clue about the eggs, but they were hard to read, especially Leroy's face. I knew it better now, but I couldn't read every look.

"I knew you shouldn't have gone on this trip," my mother said, hugging me so that I almost fell over. Davy's mom had her arm around his neck. It looked more deadly than maternal.

"I'm fine, Mom," I said. "I couldn't have asked for a better trip. Until the end." Until we gave up Alph. Until the storm. Until a tree landed on top of me.

"We saw stars," Juliette said.

Leroy nodded his head toward the door, but we couldn't get away, not yet.

"I was thinking in the car," my dad said. "That you might need some more lab space."

"Does that mean I get Juliette's room?" I said. It was bigger than mine. My sister acted like she was going to punch me, but she stopped before making contact, a sign that our relationship had improved.

"Something tells me I won't be driving that car again," my father continued. "Helluva car. If Ripley doesn't impound it, maybe I'll send it out to pasture. That would free up the garage."

Was he serious? Suddenly, it was as if he was the one who'd been struck by lightning. Maybe he was giving up on giving up. I was going to make him a new shirt for Father's Day.

"Actually," I admitted, "the Soov was dead useful. Maybe we could keep it. Outside. For emergencies. I could retrofit it with a hydrogen fuel cell engine—" I wouldn't leave the job half done, either. Maybe I'd even make a few improvements, get the Disciples to take notice.

My dad uncorked a bottle of pampas grass wine with a pop and winked at me. Then he poured it out for the adults.

Leroy caught my eye again. "Hey, Ahab. Let's go inspect your new lab space."

It hurt to lean on the crutches, so I leaned on Davy a little as we went out the side door and into the garage, where steam was still rising off the hood of the Soov. Juliette came, too, and leaned against it.

"Helluva car," she said, a perfect mimic of my dad.

Finally, we could talk. Or we could have if Derek Ripley hadn't been in the driveway, on an EPF scooter now instead of his bike. The streetlight shone behind him.

"I just came here to bring you something," he said. He pulled a thermos out of his backpack. "Varney dropped this."

Darn it, Leroy, I thought. There was no swear word strong enough. *You had one job.*

"Where'd you find it?" I tried to swallow but couldn't, like the wad of frog spawn was still in my mouth.

"He dropped it when I caught up with him," Derek said. "I almost threw it in the trash. Littering is an obvious infraction. But then I thought: No. With all the fines my dad is going to stick on your dad, you probably need all your worldly possessions. So I'd better return it."

"Well. Thanks," I said. "That was kind of you."

He shook the thermos.

"Don't!" I said.

"I think I'd better make sure there's no contraband in here. For my dad, you know?" Derek unscrewed the lid and turned the bottle upside down. I waited for the frog spawn to land in a lump on the garage floor. A few drips of water plopped out.

That's when I noticed something about the thermos: It wasn't even mine.

"It's empty," Derek said.

I dared to breathe. "Thanks for returning it," I said.

"It wasn't empty earlier," he said.

"What did you think we had in there? A lobster?" Leroy folded his arms.

Derek folded his. But there didn't seem to be anything left for him to do. He threw the thermos on the ground. Then he got on his dad's scooter and puttered back down the drive. On the rear bar, just above the license plate, I could see the EPF logo and tag line: PROTECTING THE WORLD FROM YOU; PROTECTING YOU FROM THE WORLD. They didn't do either of those things. But I guess, in his way, Derek thought he was doing his part to save the planet. That's when it hit me: *part*. Maybe we didn't have to save the whole world; maybe we just had to try to save a part of it. Even my dad had done that: He'd saved us, plus he'd kept Davy's mother from having a nervous breakdown. We'd saved Alph from being lonely, and maybe Simon, too. It remained to be seen whether or not we'd saved the bullfrogs. We were trying, and that counted for something.

"What's something times something?" I asked.

"Something squared." Delph beat Davy to the answer.

"Which is better than nothing," I said. Maybe it was the painkillers, but I grinned.

"Is he delirious?" Leroy asked.

"Mostly," Davy said.

"Hey," said Juliette as Derek disappeared in the distance. "Isn't that an infraction? Riding a scooter belonging to an EPF officer?"

"Infraction RE 7543-1," Leroy said without hesitating.

"You made that up," Delph said.

He shrugged.

"So," I said. "About that heart attack you gave me, on top of my other injuries."

"We switched thermoses," Leroy said.

"Where are the eggs?"

"Delph has them. I threw her your thermos and she threw me hers. She made an amazing catch. She could go pro, a catch like that."

"Thanks," Delph said. In the dark, I couldn't tell if she was blushing.

"Getting tossed around probably isn't good for them," Leroy said.

None of this had been good for them. But we still had them.

Delph grabbed her thermos off her bike and headed into the blackness of the backyard, toward my shed. Juliette grabbed a small ball from a bin in the garage and squeezed it once. It gave off a warm yellow light. I creaked open the shed door, and we squished inside, around the wooden plank I used as a table. Sitting on top of it was a green envelope.

At least, it looked like an envelope. It was soft, like fabric, but I hadn't felt anything quite like it before. There was no postmark and no return address, but it was from the Disciples. It had to be. Unless Davy or Leroy was playing a joke on me. But I didn't think they were. I hadn't mentioned wanting to be a D² out loud to any of my friends, except Davy. I wondered if they had envelopes at their houses, too. Or if Simon had one sitting under his plum tree.

"Dang," Davy said, even though the moment clearly called for Latin.

I opened the envelope and pulled out a small green paper,

so thin I could see through it. Three words were printed on it in gold: "Get well soon."

So it wasn't an invitation. "It's a get-well card," I said.

"But what does it *mean*?" asked Davy, who knew the possibilities.

"I guess that I should get well?" I could have spent the whole night analyzing the words for hidden meanings, enough for an A, B, C, D, E, and F. Enough to convince myself that a get-well card counted as something, too. But that would have to wait. We needed to make sure the frog spawn was safe.

Leroy and Davy prepped an aquarium, one of the bigger ones. Delph unscrewed the thermos lid. Gently, she poured the frog spawn into its new home. The pieces sat next to one another, like a puzzle.

"There," Delph said. She put the thermos on top of the table and accidentally touched my hand.

"I'm glad you're okay," she said, as if no one else was even in the shed.

I thought that might be the moment to:

(A) kiss her,

(B) find out if she wanted to be more than friends, or

(C) turn the whole thing into a game of rock, paper, scissors.

Before I could decide that kissing was the sort of thing you should save for eighth grade, Davy said: "So if we've got

American bullfrog frog spawn, but it was made in Canada, does that make them Canadian bullfrogs?"

"Actually, they're a tad Polish," Delph said. "*Tadpolish!*" she added when Leroy looked confused.

"That was terrible," I said.

Juliette said, "I hope I can frog-et it," which was also terrible. But it was perfect for her first pun.

"I can't believe after all this, I'm still going to fail social studies," Leroy said.

"We can talk to Duckworth for you," I told him. "Delphinium is very persuasive. Or Davy could just hack in and give you the grade you deserve."

"You can do that?"

Davy waved his hand. "Child's play," he said. "You deserve an A for that boat," he said. "And international travel should count for extra credit."

"My mom was right," Leroy said. "You are a good influence on me."

I thought about the thing he'd said he wanted when we were on his stoop that day: Respect. I'd only pretended to give it to him. Maybe because I was jealous. But he had it now. When I said it out loud, it felt like an apology. "Respect."

Because Leroy wasn't a bad influence either. He didn't do things the way I did them, but the things he did made my brain work differently.

Maybe I didn't even need to be a Disciple to discover great things. Maybe what I needed was my own secret society to discover things along with me.

"If the tadpoles hatch, we should tell people," I said. Just because the society was secret, it didn't mean everything had to be.

"He's delirious again," Davy said.

"They don't need to know it was us that found them—or where. Just that someone did." Seeing Leroy's lobster, even after it was recently deceased, was what got me to look for a live one. That had led me to Alph. "They need to know what's possible. If they hatch, we can show them."

"When," said Delph.

"Lots of things can happen to the eggs," I told her.

"Lots of things already did," she said.

We all looked at the frog spawn resting in the shallow water. In the heat, it would dry out in no time.

"We need water from the spring," I said.

"I'll go get some in the morning," Leroy said.

"I'll keep watch," said Delphinium.

"Let me know if you need a chaperone," said Juliette.

Leroy looked like he was still thinking about his social studies grade. "I know hanging out with a lobster murderer isn't great for your scientific reputations," he said. "I get it if you want to keep your distance in school." He'd spent the beginning of the trip trying to make us forget he'd killed a lobster. Now he was reminding us. It made zero sense. Delphinium looked at him like he was the one who was delirious.

"Did we or did we not just go all the way to Canada together to save frogkind?" she asked.

"We did."

"And did we or did we not just illegally cross the border, flee the EPF, catch a ride in a nonsanctioned vehicle, and almost get struck by lightning in a wicked storm?" Juliette added.

"We didn't almost get struck by lightning," Leroy said. "Well, except Ahab."

"You saved the frog spawn," I said. "Besides, there aren't many people in the world I would trust to help me play matchmaker for a snake."

Trust.

The answer wasn't "Trust no one," like it said in my dad's journal. The answer was to trust someone.

"Snake?" said Davy. "We're going to play matchmaker for a *snake*? *Insanis*."

I nodded, wondering if Simon could get a line on one. We'd start with the copperhead. And then whatever bird we'd heard calling that day on Alpha Island. Who knew what else was out there? There could be more lobsters or turtles or geckos, even. There could be butterflies or a moose. And okay, the moose was a long shot, but whatever was out there, we'd find it. I had a lab now. I had friends who doubled as a crack research team. And I had something else, which wasn't exactly scientific but which made all the difference anyway. I had hope.

"For the copperhead Leroy and I found the last time we were on the island," I told Davy.

"Very poisonous," Leroy added. He looked back at me. "I'm not riding to Canada with a copperhead in my backpack. But if *you* carry it, I'll keep you company."

I reached out my hand, and he reached out his. We shook. Delphinium put her hand on top of ours, and Davy and Juliette added their hands to the pile.

"Guess we have a deal, then," Leroy said.

"We have a deal," I said. But we had more than that.

We had:

(A) a partnership,

(B) a friendship, or

(C) a future.

Or maybe this was one of those times I really needed a fourth option. Because the answer that was most correct—the thing we really had—was (D) all of the above.

Acknowledgments

I wrote *One Small Hop* while bullfrogs croaked in my backyard and worries about the world and the climate took up permanent residence in my brain. Writing this book didn't calm those worries. But it did encourage me to continue thinking about things I could do to help—big, small, and in between. Helping the world is like writing, I think: The only way to get anywhere is to not give up.

Thank you to Lisa Sandell and the team at Scholastic for the careful reads and discussions and for making this book real. I have been lucky to have Wendy Wan-Long Shang as the other half of my writing brain these past few years, and I am so grateful for her "emergency reads." Thanks to Susan Cohen and Nora Long. Thanks to Paul Dellinger for giving this manuscript an early look with his sci-fi goggles, to my supportive writing group for every time they said "you're still working on the frog story, right?" and to my writing friends who led me to new discoveries. Thanks to Tom and

Cece for giving me more of a boost than they'll ever know; thank you Rachael, Anamaria, Jackie, Mary C., Mary T., Kristen, Angele, and Lenore. Thanks to "Full Blacksburg" and to everyone who walked with me, side by side and six feet apart. And thanks to my family for being who you are and for letting me be who I am. I look forward to spotting the first crocus of a new spring with all of you.

About the Author

Madelyn Rosenberg is the author of many books for young readers, including *This Is Just a Test*, a Sydney Taylor Honor Book, and *Not Your All-American Girl*, both of which she co-wrote with Wendy Wan-Long Shang. She is also the author of *The Schmutzy Family*, a National Jewish Book Award finalist; and *Cyclops of Central Park*. Madelyn lives in Arlington, Virginia. You can visit her online at madelynrosenberg.com.